The Palmetto Patriot

A STORY OF THE AMERICAN REVOLUTION

Thomas W. Lee

The Palmetto Patriot
A Story of the American Revolution

Copyright © 2025 by Thomas William Lee

All rights reserved.

P.O. Box 2884
Pawleys Island, SC 29585
www.ClassAtPawleys.com

ISBN 978-1-955095-46-4

Printed in the United States

Dedication

This book is dedicated to my father, Thomas Aloysius Lee
(1910-1993).

Like the characters in this book, he defended this country at a
time when many thought defeat was inevitable. He nearly died on
Okinawa on Easter Sunday morning in April of 1945 and returned
home with a Bronze Star and Purple Heart to resume his life at age
35.

He never spoke about his wartime experiences and his uniform
hung in his closet for more than 40 years. He died in 1993.

T.W.L.

Acknowledgments

I would like to thank several people who have advised and assisted me in the creation of *The Palmetto Patriot.*

First, to my Pawleys Island friends. Many of them read my first book, *The Chatham Patriot,* and encouraged me to write about South Carolina in the American Revolution. Without their encouragement, I might not have started this project.

In the early days of my research, I consulted with Paige Sawyer in Georgetown, South Carolina. He conducts wonderful historical walking tours, and I had worked with him previously on some genealogical photo projects. Paige got me started on the research for this book.

Paige introduced me to Robert "Mac" McAlister who has written several books on South Carolina, one of which was *Georgetown's North Island* which he published in 2015. He is a font of information and met with me. North Island is where my story begins in 1777.

My wife Denise, once again, tirelessly reviewed the final edits of the book, finding and removing my many mistakes.

Finally, I would like to thank Linda Ketron and her team at CLASS LLC. She is a pillar of our Pawleys Island Community, and she worked with me, as she does with all her authors, to make my manuscript a book that I am proud of. Her experience and knowledge of the industry were invaluable.

T.W.L.

Table of Contents

Author's Note

This book is a work of historical fiction. The main character, Samuel Huger (pronounced *You-Gee*), never existed. The characters with whom he interacts, however, were all real. In our story, Samuel has a personal perspective on the people and events that led to the founding of our country.

My first book about the American Revolution, *The Chatham Patriot*, focused on the events of 1776-1779 in New Jersey with the Battle of Brooklyn, White Plains and Springfield. It described life in the small village of Chatham, New Jersey, as those conflicts were occurring around them.

This historical marker outside of Georgetown on Highway 17 was the inspiration for this book.

My friends in South Carolina, who read *The Chatham Patriot*, encouraged me to tell the story of what happened here during those years. One day, while driving down Highway 17 to nearby Georgetown, I noticed a historical sign marker on the side of the road. I had passed it dozens of times before, noting it, but never stopping to read it. On this day, I stopped, read it, and took a picture. Lafayette arrived here in 1777? *"Why would he come here?"* I thought. My interest was piqued, and I began to do some research.

In this book, we will look more closely at "The Southern Strategy," the British plan of 1779-1781 for South Carolina. Having reached a stalemate with General Washington in the north, British General Clinton sent his fleet and army south in 1779. The plan was to take Savannah and Charleston, march north through the Carolinas and Virginia and trap Washington.

As part of my research, I visited Yorktown, Virginia, in the fall of 2024. The battlefield that those men crept across in the dark in October of 1781 is a serene pasture now. Standing at the base of Redoubt #10, where Hamilton led his men that night, made the hair on the back of my neck stand up. We can only imagine the thoughts of those young Americans at that moment so long ago.

We will examine four individuals who shaped that

Views of Yorktown battlefield and earthworks, 2024.

era: Alexander Hamilton, the Marquis de Lafayette and John Laurens, who were sometimes referred to as *"My three sons"* by George Washington, and a little understood military leader in South Carolina named Francis Marion, who was colorfully called *"The Swamp Fox"* by his British adversaries.

Alexander Hamilton has been well documented in many books and a Broadway play but what was his relationship with Washington and his fellow patriots? The most ambitious and politically astute of Washington's aides, he caught Washington's attention at the Battle of Brooklyn. He was soon at the General's side as an indispensable advisor and, later, military field commander.

The Marquis de Lafayette was an unlikely but notable figure in the American Revolution after arriving in America from France in 1777 near Georgetown, South Carolina. He went on to become one of Washington's most trusted advisors during the American Revolution and a military leader in major engagements with the British. His French lineage was instrumental in the negotiations with King Louis XVI and General Rochambeau in bringing the French Army and Navy to America's aid.

John Laurens (1732-1782), the close friend of our main character Samuel Huger, was the son of Henry Laurens, a wealthy Charleston planter. Henry owned eight plantations near Charleston and was elected President of the Continental Congress in 1777. His son John was educated in Paris, fluent in French, elected to the South Carolina legislature, joined Washington's staff with Hamilton and Lafayette as an aide-de-camp, and served as a lieutenant-colonel in the Continental Army. He fought and was wounded at Brandywine, was captured by the British in Charleston, released and sent to France to assist Ben Franklin, then returned home in time to lead a company at Yorktown in 1781. He died in 1782 in a skirmish with the British in South Carolina at a time when the Revolutionary War was effectively over. It is said that no death in the American Revolution was felt more severely by Washington than that of John Laurens.

Francis Marion (aka "The Swamp Fox") was a significant military leader in South Carolina in that era. He spent much of his youth in Georgetown and, when his brother and his wife acquired Belle Isle Plantation, just south of Georgetown, he lived there and was a successful farmer around 1770. His military exploits are legendary in South Carolina 1778-1781, 

helping to turn the tide against the British at a time when all was considered lost.

After the American General Gates was defeated at Camden in 1780 and retreated north, it was said that Marion had the only organized force remaining to stop the British march north. At times, he had as few as 50 men under his command.

Samuel Huger, our fictional main character, works closely with all four of these men and through his eyes, we will learn their story.

Other characters in our story include –

Baron DeKalb (1721-1780) was also a very real character in the story of Lafayette and the American struggle for freedom. He was of German/Prussian descent, 35 years older than Lafayette and sailed with him in 1777 to America, arriving in Georgetown, South Carolina. DeKalb's command of the English language was critical in Lafayette's early days in American since the young Frenchmen spoke very little English. DeKalb would find his own place in the Continental Army and eventually die a war hero.

Benjamin Huger (1746-1779), the father of our fictional main character, Samuel Huger, was a wealthy plantation owner outside of Charleston with a summer home/plantation on North Island just outside of Georgetown. He was the first American that Lafayette and DeKalb encountered when they rowed ashore in June of 1777. He was one of four sons of Daniel Huger, a very prominent planter and political figure in the South Carolina legislature.

Many of the other secondary characters in our story were also real.

The Allstons were wealthy plantation owners in the Georgetown/ Pawleys Island area during this time. The Allston and Marion families were closely connected by business and marriage. Both were major slave owners. Three of Francis Marion's brothers married Allston girls. One brother lived at Belle Isle Plantation in St. Stephen's Parish just south of Georgetown.

The scenes and dialog of all these historical figures' interactions that I have written about are fictional but may invite the reader to think more deeply about the role of South Carolina in America's freedom. I have done my best to capture the mood of that era in our country's history.

Fighting in the War of Independence

In telling the story of *The Palmetto Patriot*, I describe a number of battles between the British and Americans. Before delving into the story, it is useful to have a perspective on military equipment, tactics, and operations during that era.

We all know that the war was fought between America and England. Towards the end, France entered on the side of the Americans and played a major role.

England was a monarchy under King George III, with a Parliament and Prime Minister. Under King George was Lord North, the head of the British Cabinet. His Secretary of State, responsible for the war in North America, was George Germain. He had been a major general in the British Army during the Seven Years War in the 1760s. As we will see, Lord Germain was responsible for the leadership and military strategy of the British Army in America although he never once traveled to the American Colonies.

America, at that time, was a disorganized democracy without a constitution and led by a Congress representing the thirteen colonies.

The French were also a monarchy under King Louis XVI with a very strong foreign minister, Charles Gravier, Comte de Vergennes. He negotiated with Benjamin Franklin during those years and reluctantly recommended that the King support the Americans.

These two foreign ministers were instrumental in the American Revolution and neither one of them ever set foot on American soil.

The war was fought in a series of escalating events. Starting with relatively small uprisings in Lexington and Concord in Massachusetts in 1775, it steadily escalated to battles involving tens of thousands of soldiers. Neither side could have predicted the extent of the tragedy that would unfold between 1776 and 1782.

England is 3,000 nautical miles from America. To engage in a war in North America in the 1770s, England had to transport men, arms and materials by ship over the dangerous North Atlantic Ocean. England had a massive navy, and the Americans had a very minimal sea presence.

The British Navy was led by its *Ships of the Line,* the equivalent of modern-day battleships. They were massive, three-masted fighting vessels that were more than 100 yards long with three decks housing as many as 150 cannons, 75 on each side. They were all built in the British shipyards of Portsmouth and were very expensive to build and operate. They sat very low in the water because of their weight and that dictated where they could safely navigate and fight. Positioning them in battles and sieges was critical since they could only conduct "broadsides" firing of their guns at right angles to the direction they were sailing. England had about ninety of these monsters in the 1770s. France had more than one hundred.

Next were the frigates that were single deck vessels with as many as 75 cannons. Both England and France had hundreds of these fighting ships. Behind these were a large array of smaller sloops, troop transports, and supply ships of every size with smaller launches for amphibious landings.

The timing of when these ships could sail dictated the pace of the war. Due to the risk of hurricanes, you could not sail in the southern waters and Caribbean in September-October, and crossing the Atlantic in winter was risky. Throughout the war, fleets were prepared and sailed, encountering all kinds of bad weather. Trips that should have taken days ended up taking weeks or even months.

Transporting an army of several thousand men, horses, wagons, munitions, food (for both the men and their mounts), uniforms, and supplies from one place to another, required months of planning and execution. Armies would often arrive from trans-Atlantic crossings sick, malnourished, diseased and unable to fight for months after landing.

For example, in September 1777, when the British commanding officer Lord Howe decided to assault Philadelphia by sea from New York, it took him three months to prepare, and he left New York with 127 ships and 4,000 soldiers. The trip was supposed to take eight days, but they encountered fierce storms and contrary winds and it took 32 days. Most of their horses died during the trip. It took them a week to recover and by the time they landed in Maryland, the element of surprise was lost.

The lives of officers versus enlisted men were drastically different during the American Revolution. In the British Army, officers came from the upper class of wealthy, politically connected families. They would purchase a *"commission"* making them a senior officer in the King's Army. They lived a life a world apart from their men. They all rode fine horses in battle, dressed in tailored uniforms and wore white wigs. They ate well, lived in superior housing, and were treated with respect. Enlisted men in the British Army mostly came from the lower class and viewed military service as a decent paying job. They would sign on for terms of service that typically lasted five years.

There were also Americans who volunteered to serve on the British side. They were called *Tories* or *Loyalists*. Early in the war, the British Army had no use for them but as the war dragged on into the southern colonies, the British became more and more dependent on these Americans who felt that their economic well-being was dependent on a British victory. In South Carolina, the British commanders were heavily dependent on Tories. The savagery between the Loyalists and the Americans was some of the worst in the entire war.

The Americans put men on the battlefield in a very different way. To begin with, there were two different command structures. The Continental Army were the professional soldiers but, in truth, they were volunteer farm boys who signed on for only one year. They had minimal training. Throughout the war, Washington dealt with these men whose terms of service were expiring and could not be counted on. They signed on with expectations of pay from Congress but, as we will see, that contract was often not fulfilled and, at a crucial point in the war, they went on strike until they were paid.

Washington asked much of his *"Continentals."* They suffered deprivations that are difficult to comprehend. They frequently had little or no food. They lived in winter housing that was brutally inadequate in places like Valley Forge and were sometimes asked to march and fight in the dead of winter and the heat of summer. On multiple occasions, Washington, who had his military training in the British Army in the 1750s, resorted to court martials and even hangings to restore order and discipline. Through it all, they stayed with him and fought.

Alongside these Continentals were the American militia, part-time volunteers from each colonial community who signed up to defend their region. Every colony had a different arrangement with their militia and Washington was constantly in the position of *"calling up the militia."* For the most part, Washington kept the militia in a supporting role to the Continentals on the battlefield. Often, however, the militia would find themselves on the front line. At times, it would have been hard to distinguish between the two military groups.

American officers, like the British, were sourced from the upper class. Wealthy Americans like plantation owners in the south were commissioned as officers. As we will see in our story, American foreign ambassadors would sometimes offer European military men commissions in the American Army, presenting Washington with a dilemma.

Communication was a constant problem in the 1770s. Handwritten notes were given to couriers who sometimes were never able to deliver them. A note from Lord Germain in London to his military commander in New York would take at least a month to arrive.

The British commanders in America would receive their orders regarding strategy from London. They would respond, which could take another month. But British battlefield tactics in America were left up to the generals who would dispatch notes via couriers to their field commanders. Communication was sometimes also verbal and would get distorted in the heat of battle.

With communication from London taking weeks or even months, there are many examples of orders arriving too late or being ignored, as no longer relevant. For example, in New York in the summer of 1779, as Lord Howe tried to decide whether to move his forces north up the Hudson to support General Burgoyne coming down from Canada or to assault Philadelphia, an almost comical mis-timed series of notes passed back and forth between him and Lord Germain in London. He ended up sending three different proposals to London which *crossed in the mail* with contrary guidance from London coming back in the other direction. Howe decided on his own to assemble a fleet in New York and sail to Philadelphia, leading to the disastrous defeat of Burgoyne at Ticonderoga.

In another example of communications failure, the British finally decided to negotiate a cease-fire with the Americans in 1780. The English Carlyle Commission was sent to Philadelphia to negotiate a cessation of hostilities only to learn that the Americans had just signed an agreement with the French ten days earlier.

As they say, timing is everything!

Military commanders in battle in the 1770s were highly dependent on communication from their leaders. In South Carolina, communicating in the heat of battle on deploying cannons, positioning cavalry, and bringing up reinforcements would often determine outcomes. Both the British and the Americans were plagued by problems in this area.

Then there was the problem of getting troops from one place to another. The British learned a hard lesson about the geography and topography of America. Unlike European wars, the American Revolution was fought over a landscape that spanned nearly 1,000 miles from Boston to Charleston. Once in South Carolina, General Cornwallis was frustrated by the many rivers, creeks, swamps and marshes that dominated that Southern Colony. Getting his army across a seemingly insignificant creek could be a major undertaking. His American opposition, particularly the local militia, knew those waterways well and used their knowledge to great advantage.

The decision whether to transport cannons with the troops was key to the speed with which forces could move. On more than one occasion both the British and the Americans abandoned their cannons, dumping them in creeks and rivers, to move more quickly.

Marches for both armies were brutal affairs. Regiments of men walked hundreds of miles and were often too exhausted to fight once they arrived at their destination.

Food was a constant problem. Nearly every military engagement during this time has footnotes about armies foraging the local countryside for food. The British Navy on many occasions would have their on-board food lost in a storm or spoiled by insects.

Once all of this was overcome, the men would face each other on the battlefield. The officers would spend days and sometimes weeks trying to position their men in a favorable position, taking advantage of a hill or creek. The element of surprise was paramount.

Soldiers carried muskets, a single shot rifle that took about 60 to 90 seconds to reload. Men carried enough powder and ammunition for about a dozen rounds. Often, the Americans had less when ammunition ran in short supply.

The British were trained to march and fire in tight formation, with the front-line firing and reloading, while the second and third line volleyed. The effective range of what was called the smooth-bore musket was a maximum of 100 yards. Forty to 50 yards was more common. Soldiers on both sides would usually withhold fire until they could clearly see each other. Thus, the expression, popularized from Bunker Hill in 1775, "*...don't fire until you see the whites of their eyes.*"

In a documented incident at Brandywine, a British captain named Ferguson spotted a mounted Continental officer 40 yards away. Ferguson was a marksman, reputed to be one of the finest in the British Army. He described the American as follows:

"*He was a tall American officer riding a beautiful bay horse with his back to me. He briefly looked in my direction and then looked away.*"

Believing it was dishonorable to shoot a man in the back, let alone a senior officer, Ferguson did not take the shot. He was wounded the next day and related the story to his commanding officer. The Continental he spotted was George Washington. Had he not been so honorable, history might have taken a different course.

Washington learned the hard way that having his poorly trained citizen-soldiers fight using European-style battlefield formations did not work. So, the Americans fought differently from the British often hiding behind trees, earthen dikes and rock-walls, firing and then hiding while their comrades on the other side would fire their volley. This became the norm in South Carolina. The British commanders complained bitterly about these American tactics calling them "dishonorable."

"Battles" would often involve no more than seven or eight volleys before each side would withdraw to find more ammunition or a more advantageous location. They tended to be short engagements of fire, retreat, advance, and then retreat again.

Both armies' muskets were fashioned with bayonets which were put to good use when the ammunition ran out and close quarter fighting ensued. At Yorktown, for example, the Americans assaulted the British earthworks in the darkness with their muskets unloaded. They feared an accidental shot would compromise the element of surprise. The battle at Yorktown was fought hand to hand with fixed bayonets.

Disease was a constant concern. Fouled water brought dysentery and close quarters on ships and in camps advanced smallpox. More men died of disease than in battle in the American Revolution. The British had discovered the effectiveness of smallpox inoculation and, although it was primitively applied to all their men, it was 95% effective. Washington would eventually adopt smallpox inoculation, but this disease was a threat throughout the war.

Finally, the subject of prisoners should be explained. Once again, there was an enormous difference between officers and enlisted men who became prisoners of war. The 5,700 Americans who surrendered in May 1780 after the fall of Charleston are a good example.

Among the prisoners were seven American generals, multiple lieutenant-colonels, majors, captains and lieutenants. The officers, under the accepted conventions of war at the time, were soon paroled and exchanged for British officers.

While in captivity, officers had relative freedom, were well fed, and even allowed passes to visit family. For example, John Laurens, one of our main characters, was a lieutenant-colonel who was captured in Charleston and within months, released after signing an agreement he would never again take up arms against The King.

The Charleston enlisted men on the other hand were subjected to unmentionable conditions of starvation, beatings and shipped out to penal colonies in the Caribbean. Many were imprisoned on prison ships in Charleston harbor. All suffered and many died.

South Carolina in the American Revolution

America's struggle for independence from British rule has been well documented. Books and movies have depicted the many battles that were fought in Massachusetts (Lexington, Concord, Bunker Hill), New York (Brooklyn, White Plains, Saratoga, and Ticonderoga), New Jersey (Trenton, Springfield, Princeton, Monmouth), Pennsylvania (Brandywine), and Virginia (Yorktown). But the momentum of the war swung in favor of the Americans in South Carolina.

The American Revolution was fought in slow motion over the span of nearly seven years. The British Navy took sometimes as much as a year to sail across the Atlantic, once given orders. Armies walked everywhere, spent weeks positioning themselves and would sometimes withdraw without a shot being fired. Winters were spent indoors in the northeast sheltering from the harsh North American cold weather. There were many months when nothing happened on either side. A stalemate of sorts was reached in the north in 1778 after the Battle of Monmouth Courthouse when the British retreated to New York City. Washington, by then, had come to realize he could not defeat the British with conventional European-style warfare and resorted to a strategy of attack and retreat. The British, under Henry Clinton, came to a similar conclusion, deciding in 1778 to send their fleet and several thousand troops south.

What has been largely ignored, however, were the many significant and strategic battles fought in South Carolina beginning in

1778. It could easily be argued that, had the small American force in South Carolina not prevailed, the ultimate victory in Yorktown would never have happened.

More encounters with the British were fought in South Carolina than in any of the thirteen colonies. Forty-five of the 46 South Carolina counties saw action. Twenty percent of all the casualties in the American Revolution occurred in South Carolina. John Laurens, the son of a Charleston plantation owner, was a highly trusted aide to Washington, emissary to France and battlefield commander. He is reputed to be "*the last man to die in the American Revolution.*"

After substantial losses in the years 1776-1778, Washington had managed to maintain a stalemate in the north with the British generals Howe and Clinton. The South Carolina militia had repelled a British siege at Charleston in June 1776 as the ink was drying on the Declaration of Independence in Philadelphia. The British then withdrew from Charleston back to New York. Everyone expected them to return, and they did – three years later.

What emerged from all this was the British "Southern Strategy," dictated by the Foreign Minister in London, Lord Germain. The crux of this strategy was to invade and control Georgia, South Carolina, North Carolina and Virginia effectively putting Washington in a vise from north to south. It was believed the American commander would lose his popular support from the people, the black enslaved people of South Carolina would rise up against their masters, Congress would succumb to pressure from its citizens and surrender would be the only option. That was, at least, the plan.

Savannah, Georgia, mostly sympathetic to the British King, fell first as a general stationed in Florida, impatiently awaiting the arrival of the British fleet from New York, took Savannah without a shot being fired in October 1778. It would take Sir Henry Clinton, British Commander in North America, another year to get his fleet ready to sail south.

The primary target was Charleston. After a failed Continental attempt to retake Savannah in the fall of 1779, Clinton finally arrived and settled in with a massive fleet and thousands of troops, under General Cornwallis, in December. He prepared for a classic European siege of Charleston. After months of negotiations and bombardment, Charleston surrendered. Subsequent American defeats in Camden and a place called Fishing Creek seemed to seal the Americans' fate. The American commanding general, Horatio Gates, fled for his life back to Philadelphia and was stripped of his command. By the summer of 1780, it appeared that the war might end.

At that point, South Carolinians stood firm. Led by patriots such as Francis Marion, also known as "The Swamp Fox," and newly appointed General Nathanael Greene, the Continentals ever so slowly began to prevail. Marion managed to turn the tide at places not known in the history books – Nelson's Ferry, Britton's Neck, Blue Savannah and Black Mingo Creek. Ironically, some sites of Marion's most important victories are now submerged under Lake Marion, created by the Federal Government in the 1930s. It was not until late 1780 that Washington, back in Philadelphia, even heard Francis Marion's name.

The South Carolina story needs to be retold and highlighted to all students of American history. Hopefully, *The Palmetto Patriot* will contribute to that end.

Here, then, is the story of the British *Southern Strategy* of 1779 and the South Carolinians who defeated it.

Prologue ~ Charleston, June 1776

On the day that Thomas Jefferson delivered the first draft of the Declaration of Independence to Congress, a 44-year-old major in the South Carolina militia stood on the highest point of Fort Sullivan in Charleston harbor looking out to sea. Standing next to him, staring through a crude spyglass, was his commanding officer, General William Moultrie. What they saw shocked them. During the night, the British fleet under the command of Sir Henry Clinton had arrived from New York. Dozens of warships now lie at anchor, just outside Charleston harbor. As the British moved their frigates, troop transports and gun boats into position, it was obvious that they intended to attack and occupy the fort and, very likely, Charleston itself.

Sullivan's Island protected the entrance to Charleston harbor, the most valuable port of the American southern colonies. The city of Charleston was a narrow peninsula a mile from the fort within the harbor. The city was bounded by three rivers, the Ashley, the Cooper, and the Wando. Upstream on those rivers and the many creeks that fed them sat the richest plantation farms in America and the men who owned and operated them were among the wealthiest in the colonies. They produced a high-quality rice that fed millions of people in the Caribbean and Europe. They also produced a rare dye called "indigo" that was highly sought after by textile makers around the world. In fact, it was so profitable it was referred to as "blue gold" by the South Carolina planters.

The production of all these South Carolina plantations flowed across the docks of Charleston onto ships from around the world. The production engine of these plantations was slave labor and several of these plantation owners were active in the slave trade.

If Fort Sullivan were to be occupied by the British, a blockade of Charleston would be in effect, shutting down the robust economy of the south.

The militia major was Francis Marion, an unknown, inexperienced South Carolina military leader, who was charged by his commanding officer, General William Moultrie, to defend Fort Sullivan. Marion was an unlikely choice as a military officer. He was premature at birth, and it affected his development as a boy. Now in his 40s, he was five foot two, walked with a limp and weighed one hundred ten pounds. His command was the South Carolina 2nd Militia Regiment, made up of civilian volunteers. "*Raw recruits*" as Moultrie referred to them. This would be Marion's first major test as a military leader.

Moultrie continued to stare through his eyepiece at the many British ships now at anchor just a mile or two away. He finally turned to his subordinate.

"Major, we don't have much time, a couple of days at the most. Get our fortifications completed and position your men for an assault."

Marion thought for a moment.

"I have some ideas, sir, but I will need workers – hundreds of them."

"Tell me what you need, and I will put out the word."

"I need 200 blacks, wagons, saws, machetes, and bales of pine straw."

"I will contact all the plantation owners and issue the order immediately. You will get what you need."

The fort was in the final stages of construction and while the

British took several days to rest and recover from their voyage, Marion quickly got the workers he needed from nearby plantation owners who were all too happy to protect their livelihoods. Marion employed the few militia soldiers he had, along with several hundred negro slaves, to finish the fort's defenses.

During the week, American General Charles Lee arrived from Philadelphia, sent by Washington, with 200 Continental soldiers, boosting morale. But Lee and Marion immediately clashed over the fort's design and defenses. Lee was one of the most accomplished senior officers in Washington's command. He was a former British Army officer who considered his military acumen superior to even Washington himself and felt that Fort Sullivan was indefensible. His recommendation was to abandon it.

He wrote to Moultrie:

"You cannot defend this position. It is poorly designed, inadequately manned and not properly constructed. Your cannons do not have the necessary range, and your munitions and gunpowder stocks will quickly be exhausted."

Moultrie and Marion listened to this pompous former Redcoat with anger and disrespect. Although Lee outranked them as a general in the Continental Army, his formal orders from Washington did not give him the authority to overrule the local militia. Moultrie stood firm.

"Your points are noted, sir, but we have decided this is where we will make our stand. You are welcome to join us or observe."

Marion's men by then had cut down hundreds of Palmetto trees which were plentiful in the area. The slaves loaded them onto wagons and moved them to the fort. They then stacked them and packed them with sand against the exterior walls of Fort Sullivan. It was a defensive construction design, unique to the south, not seen before. Marion's militia manned their posts and waited for the assault.

It came on June 28, 1776, and it was a disaster – for the British. Without a knowledgeable Charleston harbor pilot, several British ships ran aground making easy targets for the Americans' 16-pound guns which had a range of 1,000 yards. Within an hour, they had been torn to pieces and their crews were swimming in the harbor. Then, two other British ships collided and were set on fire by the American gunners.

The British ships then opened fire on the fort. The impact of their cannon balls was absorbed by the spongy wood of the Palmetto tree trunks that Marion had stacked, with virtually no damage done to the fort's walls. Marion's strategy worked.

The British General Clinton then landed several hundred soldiers on the Isle of Palms to the north intending to wade across the narrow inlet, called "*the breach*," and attack the fort on land from the rear but the tide came in swamping the Redcoats. American sharpshooters inflicted heavy casualties on the sea-soaked British soldiers and before long, Redcoat bodies littered the beach.

Within 48 hours, Clinton gave up the fight and gave the order to withdraw. The British fleet returned to New York.

Francis Marion was hailed as a hero, promoted to Lieutenant-Colonel and the South Carolina 2nd Regiment was elevated by Congress into the Continental Army. Lee returned with his troops to the north seething at the lack of respect he was shown by Marion and Moultrie. Fort Sullivan would eventually be renamed Fort Moultrie by a proclamation of the Charleston City Council.

Calm was restored to the citizens and plantation owners of Charleston as they watched the British fleet depart. The import-export business of the plantations resumed. The British had been repelled. But one thing was clear.

They would return.

[Oller, 58]

Chapter 1 ~ Landfall, June 1777

La Victoire 1777

He was awakened in his stateroom by a gentle knock on the door.

"Oui?" he responded wiping the sleep from his eyes.

"Bon matin. Nous sommes arrivés …sir, we have arrived. We have just dropped anchor. There is a broad inlet ahead of us and we await your orders."

The 19-year-old Frenchman sat up looking around. His ship, *La Victoire*, creaked and swayed with that unmistakable on-board symphony of ropes and stays stretching and flexing with the winds. Over these past seven weeks, he had come to know that sound all too well and it was maddening – and sickening. He had suffered greatly from seasickness during the entire voyage. His name was Gilbert Lafayette d'Comte.

La Victoire was a twin-masted vessel, capable of trans-Atlantic voyages but dwarfed by the French and British man-o-war battleships so prevalent of that era. *La Victoire* was owned by Lafayette, paid for out of his substantial inheritance. The captain and crew he hired agreed to make the dangerous trip on the condition that they be allowed to take on contraband to sell to the desperate American Continental Army. Delivering Lafayette and his colleagues to America just sweetened the pot.

"Une minute, La Capitaine ….uhh, s'il vous plait, awaken Monsieur DeKalb."

His French was still heavily intertwined with his English. With the excitement now rising in him, he pulled on his breeches, his boots, his French officer's jacket and then grabbed his tri-cornered French officer's hat. He opened the stateroom door to a dark, narrow passageway and bounded up the stairs. Opening the hatch, he found himself in bright sunshine on the main deck. It was exhilarating.

His companion Baron DeKalb, a Prussian, joined him on deck with the 12 other passengers, all French Army officers. The captain silently pointed towards the shoreline. Ahead of them was a low marshy inlet that seemed to open into a broader bay. Gulls swarmed overhead and large marine animals circled at the rear of the ship. The two men took in the sight with amazement.

They had been at sea 54 days since leaving Bordeaux, France, under cover of darkness, disobeying the King of France's direct orders. Lafayette, DeKalb, and the 12 other French soldiers of fortune were in search of glory and possible fortune. The captain, who was well compensated for this voyage, managed to elude both French and British patrol boats and bring them across the Atlantic. For Lafayette, the trip had been excruciating with his seasickness. He wrote letters to his young wife Adrienne, who was pregnant back in France, stacking them in a trunk, and he remained in his cabin for much of the voyage. He used the time, however, to practice his English and read books on military tactics.

They stared at the shoreline for a very long minute before the Frenchman spoke.

"Ou sommes-nous?…uhh, where?" he said fumbling for the right English sentence.

The captain responded.

"As you know, we could not land in New York or Philadelphia as those towns are either blockaded or in British hands. Those winds we encountered pushed us much farther south and I believe we are in the Carolinas… South Carolina, north of Charleston. Charleston remains in American hands but the report we received from that American frigate we encountered two days ago was that it, too, is blockaded by British Navy gunboats." DeKalb translated all this for Lafayette.

Their original destination was hoped to be Philadelphia but the likelihood of an encounter with a British warship there was too high. All the other major American harbor entrances were blockaded by the British. Only Charleston was open, they were told. That is, until a chance encounter with an American ship two days earlier. They learned that Charleston was still in American hands after the British were defeated the previous year, but two British warships now blockaded the channel. The decision was made to sail north along the coast and drop anchor near Georgetown, some 50 miles north of Charleston.

Lafayette paused for a moment and looked through an eyepiece. He saw an inlet, framed by two sandy beaches, with grassy hills rising on both sides. He could not make out much beyond the inlet, but it appeared to open into a much wider bay.

"I believe we are looking at what the locals call North Island inlet about 50 English statute miles north of Charleston," said the captain.

The Frenchman turned and embraced his traveling companion, Baron DeKalb.

[Duncan, 46-47]

DeKalb spoke next as his English was much better than Lafayette's. "Well done, captain. Gilbert, we made it. Let's put ashore and find our American partners."

Nineteen-year-old Marquis Gilbert De Lafayette turned back to look at the shoreline.

"Vive l'Amérique" he exclaimed with a broad smile on his face.

Chapter 2 ~ Contact

The men gathered on the deck to say their goodbyes and prepare for the next phase of their journey. Lafayette and DeKalb would go first and, after making contact on shore, would send for the others.

The captain addressed them all.

"This is North Island. At the head of that inlet is a creek and that creek leads to a large American plantation. I do not know the owner, but I believe he is not a Loyalist. The port of Georgetown is close by. I have docked this ship in Georgetown on three earlier voyages and I know these people, these Americans. But I cannot trust that Georgetown is safe for us to dock. The British abandoned Georgetown some time ago but may have returned. The locals here will help you with the next step of your journey. Good luck and God-speed. I hope to make it from here into Charleston at some point."

Lafayette and DeKalb saluted the captain. They knew he wanted to get on his way to somehow deliver the remaining cargo of contraband to Charleston, making this an extremely profitable venture for him.

The plan was for Lafayette and DeKalb to make contact with the Americans and then send back for their 12 French companions. It was not known how they would be received ashore.

The longboat was lowered over the side of the French frigate and three crew members slid down the ropes to man the oars. Lafayette and DeKalb were then lowered down the ropes and took their places in the middle. Several pieces of their luggage were carefully lowered and securely stowed. One of those trunks contained letters of introduction from Ben Franklin and Silas Deane, America's envoys in Paris. The relatively small craft started to make its way toward shore. The inlet ahead was not well charted on the captain's maps, and he was unwilling to sail La Victoire through it, not knowing the depth and positions of the shoals. Running aground here, in the middle of nowhere, would be a death sentence for his ship.

The oarsmen rowed away from La Victoire and Lafayette stood, facing aft and saluted the captain who had bravely, and profitably, transported him across the Atlantic to America.

They caught a following breeze through the inlet and unfurled a small sail. They entered the inlet and sailed north, looking for the entrance to that creek the captain had described. Long scaly animals with large teeth lined the beach on both sides. A couple of them slid into the water following the boat for a few minutes. They found the creek, sailed into it and before long they encountered another sailboat. There were six negroes aboard casting and dragging their nets. Lafayette instructed that his sail be lowered so that they could talk to these men. The Frenchmen approached cautiously but it was clear that the black men were not armed and, most likely, servants of the local plantation owner.

As the boats neared, Lafayette could see fear in the men's eyes. The men in both boats exposed their palms to each other indicating no weapons. One of the negroes spoke French and Lafayette directed the discussion. After a couple of exchanges with him, Lafayette turned to DeKalb and the oarsmen.

"These men are owned by the master of an American plantation here. There is a narrower creek up ahead and that will lead us to the main house."

The channel narrowed to the creek that the oystermen had described. Before long, they were alongside what appeared to be cultivated, flooded fields with earthen dikes and a wooden dam controlling the water level. Lafayette had read about these rice field floodgates but had never seen one. It was now late in the day and the shadows were lengthening. Beyond the dam, several black workers could be seen, knee deep in the water of the fields. This was undoubtedly one of the many rice and indigo plantations of South Carolina that Lafayette had read so much about.

Lafayette, a product of French aristocracy, had not yet thought much about the incredible contradiction of American liberty and African slavery. For now, he just saw these men as servants, much as he had seen countless servants in French society. In France, Lafayette had grown up in a society of servants but the notion of slaves, owned by another person, was something he had only read about. Here it was now, right in front of him.

Immediately, a white man appeared, tall and rangy with knee high boots. He was the plantation overseer. What dominated the scene, however, was the musket he carried, lowered somewhat at the approaching longboat.

"Halt right there," he shouted. "State your business."

Lafayette arose from his seat and the man raised the musket, pointing it at Lafayette. DeKalb intervened in English.

"Sir, we come in peace. We are Frenchmen who come to America to," he paused, searching for the correct word, "assist in the American war for freedom."

This was not a response the overseer had expected. He paused for a moment taking in the scene.

"Come closer and let me inspect your boat."

A moment or two later, he lowered his weapon.

"Continue up this creek and you will find a dock. Tie your boat up there and I will meet you. Mind the gators don't get you."

"Gators?"

Chapter 3 ~ Arrival

It was late June 1777, and the day had been like all the others this summer. The rhythms of life on the Huger Plantation were dictated by the sun, the winds, and the tides. This was the Huger summer plantation home on North Island, South Carolina.

Samuel Huger was 22, having just completed his studies in Charleston and Philadelphia. To be honest, he wanted to be anywhere other than here. At school, he had a taste of American city life, and it appealed to him. He had met some important people in Philadelphia, and Samuel had an emerging sense that he was destined to do some important things. Growing rice and indigo in South Carolina were not among them. There were daily reports from the north about the war, and Samuel longed to be a part of the fight. His father was an officer in the South Carolina militia but had held his son back from enlisting.

His father had put him to work this summer in one of the marsh fields, preparing it for next year's rice plants, and Samuel oversaw the work of 12 of their negro servants. The workday ended a little early and Samuel walked back with the workers. They hit the fork in the road. To the left was the Huger summer plantation house. To the right, were the workers' quarters. Samuel shook hands, waved goodbye and veered off to the left. As he watched them walk away, he could only wonder about these men and their lives as slaves to his father. A couple of them were his age but, unlike Samuel, they had no future.

It was now late afternoon, and he returned to the house to prepare for dinner.

As he was climbing the stairs to his room, he heard the overseer ride up on horseback and talk to his father on the front porch. Benjamin Huger nodded, quickly grabbed his rumpled hat and headed towards the dock. Two of his manservants from the house followed carrying muskets. Samuel followed all of them down the dirt path.

This was Benjamin Huger's summer residence, a sprawling 1,800-acre rice plantation just north of Georgetown on North Island. His primary home was a plantation he inherited from his father, Daniel Huger, on the Cooper River just north of Charleston. Daniel Huger, Samuel's grandfather and a prominent South Carolina political figure, had passed his holdings to his four sons in 1770.

The Hugers were of French descent. Their ancestors were Huguenots, protestants in Catholic France, one hundred years earlier. Persecuted by Louis XIV for their beliefs, thousands left France and settled in western South Carolina hoping to find religious freedom.

This North Island enterprise was where Benjamin spent the last five summers, developing and expanding his rice and indigo growing enterprise and teaching his son, Samuel, the business of running a plantation. His wife had succumbed to smallpox several years earlier so this plantation was now his major focus. The Hugers' business was very good, and profits were strong but some recent British incursions into South Carolina had been disruptive.

A staunch supporter of American independence, Benjamin Huger had recently accepted a commission in the South Carolina militia carrying the rank of colonel and commensurate with his financial status in Charleston. All his brothers were also commissioned officers in the militia. His brother, Isaac Huger, was a general in the South Carolina militia. With the British focusing mostly on military actions up north, the South Carolina militia was mostly engaged in slave uprisings and some upstate civil insurrections of

Huguenots against their Scotch-Irish neighbors. With the British Army mostly gone, the lowcountry was getting back to business-as-usual.

Father and son stood on the dock watching the approaching vessel. One oddly dressed man was standing in the bow of this longboat. The oars were raised and the longboat bumped against the dock. Ropes were tossed to the negro servants on shore and the vessel was secured to the bulkhead.

Lafayette stepped up onto the dock and DeKalb followed, their first steps on American soil. Lafayette decided to do the talking now.

"Bonjour, hello, my name is Gilbert Marquis De Lafayette and this is my compagne – uh, companion, Monsieur Baron DeKalb. We have just arrivés ... err, arrived ... from France with ..." a long pause ...

"... commissions in the American Army ... from your American ambassadors in Paris. We are here to fight for your ... independence. We are accompanied by 12 more commissioned officers from France, currently aboard our ship, *La Victoire*, to enlist in your fight for liberty."

With that said, Lafayette and DeKalb removed their hats and bowed towards the two Americans before them.

Huger looked at his son, Samuel, and raised one eyebrow. These two Frenchmen, wearing dirty military uniforms, presented quite a sight. The Frenchman doing all the talking looked like a pasty-faced young boy. He was nothing like Huger's son, Samuel, who was tall and tanned. The other guy, Baron something, was a middle-aged man with greying hair at his temples. An unlikely couple to say the least. Their offer to fight for American independence was a bit preposterous.

Huger motioned to the two servants holding muskets to lower them. This pair clearly posed no threat.

"Well, sir, my name is Benjamin Huger, the proprietor of this plantation, and I am a colonel in the South Carolina militia. This is my son, Samuel. Welcome to this extension of Huger Plantation."

Huger turned to the servants. "Bring their bags to the cottage."

Turning back to the two men.

"Come with me to the house and tell us your story."

Chapter 4 ~ Introductions

The four men sat in the spacious front room of the Huger summer house. The sun was low in the western sky behind the trees, casting long shadows over the house which faced the ocean some two miles away, across the marsh. Fortunately, a brisk breeze was pushing the hot humid air inland, and the room was quite comfortable. A negro maid brought some tea sweetened with molasses.

"Dinner will be in one hour, Mastah Huger."

"Thank you, Louise."

"So, Mr. LaFayette. We are intrigued by your story. You certainly have come a long way."

"Oui, monsieur." Lafayette kept accidentally sliding back into French.

"I am the son of Michel de Lafayette who died at the Battle of Minden when I was a young boy, and I have been an officer in King Louis' Army for several years. My father-in-law is Monsieur Le Noailles, le duc d'Ayen in the Court of King Louis."

Given the young man's age, it was obvious to Benjamin and his son that the Frenchman was stretching the truth about his length of service. He went on for several minutes about his family and the wealth he was inheriting. He told of meeting Silas Deane and Ben Franklin in Paris. Huger knew that Deane was the Continental Congress' emissary to the Court of Louis XVI and Franklin was replacing him. Lafayette continued.

"I have been passionate about your fight for liberty from the British, and Monsieur Deane, in his capacity as American ambassador, conferred upon me, Monsieur DeKalb and my 12 colleagues aboard *La Victoire* commissions in your Continental Army. My king, Louis, supports my journey here and my goal of fighting for your independence."

Lafayette was nothing if not skilled in the art of exaggeration and persuasion, sometimes known as lying. He neglected to fill in his host on some key details. Despite being 19, he was married with an infant child back in France. His young wife was Adrienne de Noailles, daughter of the duke de Noailles, an extremely wealthy and influential man in the French palace. Lafayette's marriage, at age 16, was one of opportunity and put him in position to inherit an enormous fortune. Lafayette was also careful to omit the fact that Silas Deane was being replaced by Benjamin Franklin for having significantly overstepped his authority in France. Granting dozens of opportunistic French fortune hunters American military commissions was just one example of that. Also, Lafayette's military experience was mostly ceremonial, although he was in one limited engagement with the British during The Seven Years War. Lastly, he neglected to inform the Hugers that King Louis had recently issued an edict forbidding French military officers from serving in the American Continental Army. The year 1777 was a difficult time economically and politically in France, and Louis was trying to appease the British King George III and avoid an expensive war. There was certainly no love lost between the French and the British, but neither was in a position to initiate new hostilities in 1777.

All Benjamin Huger knew was that he had a Frenchman and a Prussian sitting in his home, with 12 more men a few miles away, declaring their commitment to the American cause. Who was he to deny them? The question of the legitimacy of their commissions would be a matter for Washington or Congress to determine.

Young Samuel Huger spoke up.

"So, how can we help you?"

"We need to make our way to Philadelphia to join Washington."

The elder Huger thought for a minute and responded

"Well, sirs, I admire your ambition but you will need a heavy course of resolve. Philadelphia is some distance from here and things are not going well up there."

They spoke for another hour when Louisa rang a small bell.

"Gentlemen, let us eat. We will send for your colleagues in the morning. I hope you like wild turkey."

Lafayette nodded and DeKalb smiled.

"Sir, I have one question. What is a 'gator'?"

The two Huger men laughed out loud.

"You Europeans have much to learn about America!"

Chapter 5 ~ Georgetown

The dinner was something Lafayette and DeKalb had never experienced. Plates of white and brown turkey meat, sweet potatoes, mountains of rice and something called collard greens, along with several bottles of wine were all served.

During dinner, Colonel Huger related the stark realities of the American fight with the British. After driving the British out of Boston in 1775, British General Howe arrived back in New York a year later with 500 ships and 40,000 men. He overwhelmed Washington in the Battle of Brooklyn, killing hundreds and capturing thousands of Americans. Washington barely escaped to fight on and, despite his surprise victory in Trenton and Princeton on Christmas 1776, the news was not good. The British Navy controlled New York and access to the ports of Baltimore, Wilmington, and Charleston. The Americans were in desperate need of military supplies and despite the willingness of several European countries to assist, the British had effectively cut off "the colonies" from the world with their blockade.

In South Carolina, the situation was somewhat different. In 1776, the British had been chased out of Georgetown without a shot being fired and the Continentals had repulsed a British landing at Sullivan's Island in Charleston harbor. The British left small garrisons around the state but everyone expected they would eventually return in force.

Charleston seemed to be oblivious to the larger war situation, and life went on as usual there with balls and parties. Business was very good on the surrounding rice plantations trading with France, Spain, and the Caribbean islands. At times, even a Chinese ship put into port.

Times were good and the society life seemed to supersede the war environment "up north."

Samuel had spent two years studying in Charleston at the new College of Charleston and then two more years in Philadelphia at the University of Pennsylvania. He had earned his degree and returned to work with his father. During the dinner, Samuel had many details and insights to share about both cities. Lafayette and DeKalb were fascinated by this articulate young man.

Dinner ended and Benjamin Huger concluded the night.

"I hope you and your oarsmen are comfortable this evening in our guest cottage. We will send for your colleagues in the morning."

At breakfast the next morning, fruit and sweet breads were served with coffee and tea. Lafayette and DeKalb once again ate heartily.

Benjamin Huger rose from the table and announced,

"I have decided your best course of action is to travel to Charleston. But traveling by ship would expose you to capture by British war vessels and I am sure they would love to get their hands on a group of French military officers. You will travel overland. My son is familiar with the route and will accompany you. From there, you can secure passage either by land or sea to Philadelphia. I have sent for the best harbor pilot in Georgetown to take your ship to Charleston. With any luck, your captain can slip by the British blockades into Charleston harbor. In the morning, you will go to Georgetown to secure arms and supplies for your trip south."

The rest of Lafayette's party arrived later that day, and they began preparations to travel to Georgetown and then on to Charleston.

In the morning, they left for Georgetown only three miles away. Georgetown was a quiet little port at that time but was the main conduit of the local plantations' rice and indigo crops to Europe and the Caribbean. Major plantations owned by families like the Allston's shipped their products out of the Georgetown harbor. Throughout the war for independence, it would alternatively be occupied and then abandoned by British troops. At present, the British were gone with only a few outposts in the interior of the upstate.

They took a ferry across the bay and made their way to Georgetown. They walked down Front Street alongside sloops and frigates of all sizes that were either being loaded or unloaded. At the general store, they purchased two wagons, horses, weapons, tents and provisions for their journey.

At dinner that evening in Georgetown, Lafayette approached Samuel.

"You know, Samuel, you should consider traveling with us to Philadelphia. A man of your intelligence would be valuable to Washington."

"Let me think about it." As it turned out, he had already thought about it.

Something about the way Lafayette described it resonated with Samuel. He knew he wanted to do something beyond becoming a rice planter. He loved his time in Philadelphia at the college there, so maybe returning made sense. A few minutes later, he spoke.

"I will accompany you, but I must talk to my father. I will go back to North Island in the morning and return tomorrow evening."

The group ate in Georgetown that evening and in the morning, Samuel borrowed a horse from a merchant his father knew, rode out to the inlet and took the ferry back to North Island. There were two stops he needed to make. He stopped by the Huger summer house first and found his father reading a newspaper from New

York – *Rivington's Gazette*. It was a pro-British publication and his father was frowning.

Benjamin Huger looked up.

"You are back so soon?"

"Father, I have made a decision I must tell you about. I will be accompanying our visitors to Philadelphia. Once there, I am not sure what my plans will be."

His father frowned, processing this news, and what it meant to the Huger plantation. He removed his glasses that were perched on the end of his nose and looked at his son. Samuel was a tall, ambitious young man now. But Benjamin Huger was thinking about their plantations. He thought for a long minute.

"Okay, son, I will carry on here without you and get your younger brother more involved, but I will need you back here at some point. My role in the militia is likely to escalate, taking me away from our family business and you will have to step in soon."

Samuel didn't say anything but at age 22, running this plantation was not in his future plans. The father and son talked for a few more minutes about the war "up north."

Samuel hugged his father and left. Benjamin Huger watched his son ride away with a slight sense of jealousy at the boy's sense of adventure.

Samuel's second stop was at the neighboring Allston plantation.

He needed to say goodbye to Rebecca Allston, but he was not entirely sure what he would say. A young man arriving unannounced to see the daughter of a plantation owner was something you just did not do in 1777. He was breaking all the social rules of protocol and etiquette.

He rode up and handed the reins of his horse to a negro who was tending the front garden. Arriving on the porch, he encountered one of Rebecca's younger sisters, but he could not remember her name. He told her he was there to see Rebecca and the young girl gasped a little and ran into the house. He stepped inside the door to a large foyer. It was a hot steamy day, and the house had almost no air circulating.

In a couple of minutes, Rebecca's father, John Allston, appeared pulling his coat on despite the heat. He started to scold Samuel for this unannounced intrusion but then Rebecca's mother came down the stairs and intervened.

"Oh, shush, John. This nice Huger boy is here to see our daughter."

Mrs. Allston over emphasized the French pronunciation of Samuel's last name, YOU-GEE.

They instructed a house maid to bring Samuel to the rear porch overlooking the bay. The breeze there was marvelous. A pitcher of water was placed on a small table and Samuel gulped down a glass, staring across the marsh fields out towards the ocean.

Samuel waited a few minutes and Rebecca soon appeared. She had obviously tried to look prepared, but she clearly was surprised. She motioned him to sit with her on the couch. Rebecca's mother and sister hovered a short distance away.

"Samuel, so nice to see you," she said, offering her hand for him to kiss. They had met a few years earlier, and Samuel had seen her from time to time at various family social functions. Since he had returned from school, he had sent small signals of his interest in her.

"To what do I owe this surprise visit?"

Samuel stammered a bit to explain himself. He had been with quite a few women in Philadelphia during his university days, but this was different. Rebecca was an Allston and that meant she was part of an elite, upper class of rice planter families. Her father owned the largest plantation in what was called the lowcountry, north of Charleston.

Samuel launched into the story of Lafayette and DeKalb, the excursion to Charleston, and the plan to travel to Philadelphia. He then spoke about the war and British oppression, of which the Allstons were acutely aware. Rebecca's father was heavily involved in providing contraband, at a profit of course, to the Continental Army.

Samuel was nervous and Rebecca was clearly confused. He finally got to the point.

"Rebecca, you and I have met only a few times, but I have enjoyed our discussions. I hope you think well of me. I will be accompanying some Frenchmen to Philadelphia and hopefully joining Washington's forces against the British. I hope to return when it's all over, but I don't know when. May I write to you while I am gone?"

Asking permission to write to a young woman was a formal step forward in 1777.

She smiled and said, "Yes," barely letting him finish the sentence.

He smiled and wanted to kiss her but that would be way over the line. Maybe at one of the social houses or bars in Philadelphia but not here in proper South Carolina. Mrs. Allston suppressed a smile from the other end of the porch. Rebecca's younger sister giggled.

Impetuously, he reached in and kissed her cheek, causing a gasp from Rebecca's mother and a smile from Rebecca.

He stood, formally bowed and went back through the house to his waiting horse out front. As he rode away, Mrs. Allston said, "What an impetuous young man!"

"Yes, mother, he certainly is."

Samuel confirmed to Lafayette at dinner that evening in Georgetown his decision and the Frenchman responded with one word.

"Bon!"

They were ready. They would leave in the morning for Charleston, the first step on the way to Philadelphia.

Chapter 6 ~ Charleston

Samuel Huger decided they would take the coastal route, explaining that the terrain would be sandier, but an inland route would expose them to more danger. Roving bands of escaped slaves were robbing and sometimes killing travelers. The trip should take three to four days.

At camp each night, Samuel and Lafayette would stay up talking. Samuel was fascinated by this Frenchman's resolve and idealistic determination to fight for America and Lafayette was impressed by this American's easy style and knowledge of the American colonies. Lafayette's English was still poor but Samuel could understand the conversation with DeKalb doing the translating. Each young man was highly educated, and their discussion was at times intense. They immediately bonded.

The trip was grueling but uneventful. The loaded wagons bogged down in the sand and the heat was almost unbearable. Three days later the group arrived in Charleston looking somewhat disheveled. The locals were in disbelief of their story and showed them no affection. Samuel's time there at the college was of great help but none of the local officials greeted them or offered assistance. Samuel had to find them lodgings and more supplies for the next step of their journey.

[Duncan, 48-50]

Then *La Victoire* arrived. Strong gusty winds had pushed the British blockade frigates out to sea, and Lafayette's ship, with the help of the harbor pilot, managed to enter under cover of darkness. Once the captain told his story, Charleston's elite immediately changed their attitude towards these Europeans.

A dinner was arranged in their honor and for the next week, they were feted and toasted for their support of America's cause. DeKalb, as a veteran European military officer, agreed to inspect the city's defenses, and Lafayette even arranged with some bankers to purchase and donate some munitions to the city.

The Charlestonians, however, would prove to be duplicitous over time. In a couple of years, when challenged by British forces, they would acquiesce and declare neutrality in an effort to preserve their way of life.

Lafayette quickly sold his ship to a planter's agent who immediately outfitted it for exporting rice and indigo. The proceeds of the sale enabled Lafayette to purchase more horses and wagons needed for the two-week trip north to Philadelphia.

That night, Lafayette wrote to his wife Adrienne, back in France, *"My own reception has been most peculiarly agreeable. To have been merely my traveling companion suffices to secure any of our men the kindest welcome. I have just passed five hours at a large dinner given in compliment to me by a gentleman of this town. Generals Howe and Moultrie, as well as several officers of my suite, were present. We drank each other's health and endeavored to talk English, which I am beginning to speak a little. Tomorrow I shall pay a visit in company with these gentlemen to the governor of the state and make last arrangements for my departure. The next day the commanding officers here will take me to see the town and its environs and I shall then set out to join Washington's army. I have met a young American who has agreed to be my guide and companion. Give my love to our precious Anastasie. Gilbert."*

Chapter 7 ~ The Trip to Philadelphia

Nothing about the trip to Philadelphia went as planned. They left in late July in the sweltering South Carolina summer heat, and they were plagued by torrential thunderstorms and swarms of insects. The wagons they had acquired proved inadequate for the rough roads and deep mud. Several horses died and had to be replaced. There were times when the whole group despaired, except for Lafayette. He displayed leadership and determination under the most extreme conditions. Samuel had made this trip several times, traveling to his college in Philadelphia. He was used to more luxurious accommodations in a fine carriage with manservants.

They arrived in Wilmington in six days and Norfolk a week later. One night, thieves sneaked into their camp and stole some of their baggage. Samuel wanted to track them down, but Lafayette checked to see if the trunks with his uniform and letters of recommendation were still there. Once he was assured of that, he told Samuel,

"Let them go. What they took can easily be replaced and they probably need those clothes more than we do."

Next, they rested and resupplied near Yorktown, Virginia, careful to avoid the small, local British garrison. Lafayette wrote several letters to his wife and father-in-law back in France. Regular commercial shipping from Yorktown would ensure those letters reached their destinations. Samuel decided not to send any more letters to his father for fear of aggravating him even further.

But he did write to Rebecca.

"My dearest Rebecca,

We have arrived in Virginia on our way to Philadelphia. Our party is much beleaguered. My French companions are unaccustomed to these conditions, but M. Lafayette is proving to be a capable traveler. Our mission is clear and once in Philadelphia we will be assisting Washington in our great American struggle.

Please be safe and I look forward to seeing your countenance once again.

Yours – Samuel."

He reread it three times to ensure it did not seem too forward. He reconsidered the word "yours." He thought of discarding it but finally handed it to a ship captain's courier and handed him a few coins for his service.

Little did they all know they would return to Yorktown under very different circumstances in four years' time. For the rest of the journey north to Philadelphia, they enjoyed good weather – hot and sultry but clear. They arrived in Philadelphia in mid-August 1777.

Chapter 8 ~ No Respect

The party of 13 Frenchmen, one Prussian, and one American found a boarding house that Samuel Huger knew of from his college days. It was owned by a friend of his grandfather. The Hugers had relationships with wealthy individuals throughout the colonies due to their extensive Charleston trading businesses.

Once settled, they sat down one evening to map out their plan for approaching General Washington. They quickly learned that Washington was at his headquarters camp in Morristown, New Jersey but was expected to return to Philadelphia soon. In fact, there were indications that most of the Continental Army was moving south for some unknown reason.

It was a Sunday, and the Continental Congress was not yet in session. They randomly selected John Hancock as the first congressman they would approach on Monday morning. They would let Samuel, the wealthy southern American, do the introduction, and then Lafayette and DeKalb would make their plea for an introduction to Washington.

Their timing could not have been worse. What they did not know was that an enormous British force had recently sailed out of New York. Washington had two, well placed spies in Elizabethtown, New Jersey, where the ships were being loaded. Two of Washington's spies, one of whom was a negro named Ben, had infiltrated the dock crews and learned the fleet was heading to Philadelphia. Washington was planning to engage them somewhere outside of the city. Congress was already considering evacuation to the interior of Pennsylvania.

The meeting with Hancock was abrupt. He basically told them this was not his area of responsibility and closed the door in their face.

Several other visits to prominent members of Congress ended the same way. Clearly, they needed another strategy.

Chapter 9 ~ John Laurens

They were at their wits' end. They had not even had the opportunity to present their case, much less argue for their commissions' rank. On the sixth night in Philadelphia, Samuel, Lafayette and DeKalb went to dinner at one of the popular restaurants, The City Tavern. They were all discouraged but Samuel thought they should experience the Philadelphia that he knew when he was a student there. Lafayette missed his wife and family and was talking about them. DeKalb, as usual, was quiet and stoic over dinner.

A well-dressed young man entered, engaged in deep discussion with two older men. They were seated a few tables away, just out of earshot. Their conversation was intense, and Samuel was immediately impressed with the young man. He was gesticulating and the two older men seemed to be listening closely to his every word. Samuel inquired from their barmaid if she knew him.

"Oh, yes, everyone knows John Laurens, the son of Henry Laurens, President of the Continental Congress."

The Laurens family was well known to Samuel in South Carolina, although he had never met John. Henry Laurens had recently been elected as president of the Continental Congress and just arrived in town with his son. The Laurens were one of the preeminent families in Charleston and Samuel's grandfather had been a close friend of Henry Laurens when Henry presided over the Charleston Provincial Congress. The Laurens and Huger families were both wealthy plantation owners and active political figures in South Carolina.

Samuel observed John Laurens as different men came to his table to shake his hand and engage him in short conversations. He was strikingly handsome and seemed to possess a poise and presence well beyond his years.

Samuel, Lafayette and DeKalb watched and waited for an opportunity to approach him. Going directly to members of the Continental Congress had yielded nothing thus far so perhaps this son of an influential congressman could help.

Laurens' two older companions departed and, as he finished his meal, he was elegantly holding a glass of wine.

Samuel got up. "Let me handle this."

Lafayette and DeKalb watched as their American companion approached Laurens. They shook hands and had a pleasant conversation. Laurens motioned Samuel to sit down and they spoke for a few more minutes. Then Laurens stood and walked with Samuel to their table.

Samuel did the introduction.

"Messieurs – the Marquis de Lafayette and Baron Dekalb, allow me to introduce John Laurens, fellow citizen of South Carolina."

Lafayette and DeKalb stood and bowed and, at this point, most of the patrons in the restaurant were looking on. Laurens smiled and motioned for them all to sit. These four men, three in their twenties and one in his fifties, began to talk. To Samuel's surprise, Laurens began in perfect French. The conversation went on for a couple of minutes when Laurens turned to Samuel,

"But we are being rude to my fellow South Carolinian. Let us continue in English."

With that, Lafayette began to plead his case, in broken English, describing Silas Deane's Paris commissions and their fervent desire to aid the American cause. He spoke about their arrival in Georgetown, meeting Benjamin and Samuel Huger, Charleston, and the arduous trip north.

Laurens took this all in. Here were two Europeans, military officers, who traveled thousands of miles with a dozen other likeminded companions, at their own expense, to volunteer their services to Washington.

He ordered another bottle of wine. John Laurens articulately laid out the American situation and the role his father was playing in the Continental Congress. He, too, desired to join the fight but his father was holding him back, expecting his son to be a lawyer in Philadelphia.

Laurens told them that their sponsor in Paris, Silas Deane, was not well regarded by Congress and was being replaced by Benjamin Franklin. His advice, "Don't mention Silas Deane by name."

Washington's military situation in August 1777 was not desperate but it was precarious. The rout at the Battle of Brooklyn the previous year was still fresh on everyone's mind, despite the victories at Trenton and Princeton. And now, word was spreading that Howe's forces had left New York for Philadelphia.

"Gentlemen, I am impressed with your fervor and determination. I will speak to my father in the morning and give you a chance to convince him. You have made a good choice in allowing a South Carolinian like Samuel to speak on your behalf."

With that, he looked at Samuel and tipped his glass.

They all toasted, and the conversation turned to the beauty of the various barmaids in this restaurant. They said their goodbyes well after midnight.

As they watched John Laurens climb into his father's personal carriage, Samuel said what they all were thinking,

"Well, this was certainly an interesting evening."

Chapter 10 ~ Henry Laurens

Henry Laurens was busy trying to evacuate his new office across the street from the rooms where the Continental Congress met. He had no sooner arrived in Philadelphia to preside over the Continental Congress, when Washington ordered the evacuation. Having been elected President a few months earlier, Henry began settling his plantation and export business affairs in South Carolina. He and his son made the arduous 800-mile journey to Philadelphia together, along with several slaves as bodyguards and manservants. Henry Laurens learned, during this journey, that his son had become an abolitionist during his time in Europe. The dichotomy of that situation was not lost on one of the largest slave owners in America. They traveled at the same time as Huger and Lafayette but under much more comfortable conditions. They all had arrived in Philadelphia in early August 1777.

Congress was meeting the next day and Henry Laurens was working on his speech. He also had plans for reestablishing the Congress at a safe distance from Philadelphia. His son, John, bounded in with a big smile on his face.

"Father, it is good to see you working on the affairs of state so early this morning."

The elder Laurens did not even look up from his speech. He was annoyed at this intrusion, even if it was his son.

"I am busy, John. I am sure you have heard we must evacuate."

"There are some people I want you to meet. They are outside now."

"Absolutely not. I told my aides no visitors this morning."

With that said, the father and son began talking simultaneously. This went on for thirty seconds.

"Samuel Huger is outside now and I will bring him in. He will be brief."

"But ..."

John Laurens opened the door and in stepped 22-year-old Samuel Huger. Henry Laurens knew the Huger family back in Goose Creek, South Carolina, and they had several business dealings involving trade and slaves.

Samuel stepped forward and extended his hand causing an exasperated Laurens to stand and shake it. The elder Laurens knew this young man's father, uncles and grandfather, as all were major plantation owners near Charleston.

Samuel began,

"I will be brief, sir, as I know these are critical times. There are men outside who can help our cause – military men from France. They carry recommendations from Silas Deane in Paris. They have traveled here at their own expense and seek no compensation."

The Deane reference was a non-starter and Henry raised his eyebrows. But that last part caught his attention. Frenchmen had been cycling through Philadelphia for weeks, seeking lofty titles and significant salaries in return for service to America. Washington was fed up, and he recently had written a letter rejecting all recommendations from Deane.

Laurens realized the only way to get this over was to meet these two.

"All right, dammit, send them in."

John Laurens and Samuel Huger stepped aside. The Marquis de Lafayette and Baron DeKalb stepped into the room and stood before the President of the Continental Congress.

DeKalb stepped forward first, bowed and said in perfect English, "I am honored, sir."

Lafayette did the same, but he lapsed into French.

"Je suis honoré."

The American leader listened to their story. He had heard it before from others. He was not very impressed with the youthful Frenchman but his family did have connections in the court of Louis XVI.

The Prussian was another matter. He seemed like a man of substance and military experience. After several minutes, as much to end this meeting as anything else, he agreed to take it up with Washington.

As they shook hands to depart, Henry Laurens said, "Now, understand, no promises."

Chapter 11 ~ Laurens and Washington

Later that afternoon, Henry Laurens met with Washington. The two men knew each other socially but were not close friends. Both were owners of large plantations, both bought and sold slaves, and both were very wealthy. Most importantly, both had bound their fame and fortune to the American cause.

They had many serious matters to discuss, not the least of which was the evacuation plan for Congress should British General Howe bring his men and ships to the Philadelphia waterfront.

As the meeting was ending, Laurens said to the General, "Sir, there are two other matters I wish to discuss. Both involving your personal staff. I would consider it a personal favor if you would accept my son John as an interim aide-de-camp until you fill your open positions. Hamilton needs more capable men to assist you. My boy has foolish notions of military glory, and I need to keep him out of harm's way."

Washington nodded.

"Second, sir, there are two recently arrived Europeans who might be of service. A Prussian named DeKalb who is an experienced line officer, and a youngster named Lafayette. This young Frenchmen's family has connections to the Court of King Louis which we might be able to exploit at some point. What's more, he seeks no compensation. Another French-speaking member of your staff might prove useful if Franklin can make progress in Paris.

"The Prussian is an easy decision, assign him as lieutenant-colonel and give him a small field command. We could sorely use some battlefield experience."

Washington grunted and waved his hand signing the two appointments that Laurens put before him. It was important to get this South Carolinian in his corner and these seemingly trivial appointments cost nothing. They would, however, turn out to be two of the most important decisions he would make as commander-in-chief.

In a short time, Washington would refer to *"my three sons – Hamilton, Lafayette and Laurens."*

Washington, ever the politician, sent John Laurens the following note:

"If you will do me the honor to become a member of my Family, you will make me very happy, by your company and assistance in that line as an extra aid and I shall be glad to receive you in that capacity whenever it is convenient for you. Your most humble servant,

G. Washington."

[Unger, 46]

John Laurens breathlessly read the letter to Samuel Huger and the two embraced.

"Samuel, you must join me. I will secure a lieutenant's commission for you, and we will fight together."

This is what Samuel had been waiting for – a chance to get in on the action against the British. He eagerly agreed and within a week, he had his commission and officer's lapels as a courier and aide on Washington's staff. It was not a field command, but it was a start.

That night, Samuel wrote letters to his father and to Rebecca telling them of his new adventure. He was not sure how either of them would receive the news. His note to Rebecca was a bit self-indulgent.

"Rebecca – I hope you are well on North Island. I have made it to Philadelphia and have just been commissioned as a lieutenant in the Continental Army. I will be advising Washington himself on matters of war and diplomacy.

I long for the time when I can return and talk with you about our families and homes and beautiful South Carolina.

Take care.

Yours, obediently, Samuel."

The appointments and commissions of Lafayette and Huger took a couple of weeks but Washington made it happen.

George Washington now had three aides-de-camp, all very young – Alexander Hamilton, John Laurens, and the newly arrived Frenchman, the Marquis de Lafayette. Samuel Huger was their attaché at their right hand every day.

Chapter 12 ~ The Three Aides

Those first few days were hectic. It was confirmed that Howe was coming to Philadelphia and the Congress was leaving. Hamilton was slightly annoyed that Washington had added these men to his staff without conferring with him, but he would quickly come to appreciate their ideas and talent.

These three young men, ranging in age from 19-22, would exert enormous influence on the events of the next five years. They were from completely different backgrounds and circumstances. Despite their age, two were married men with children. War had separated them from their families.

Hamilton grew up on the Caribbean Island of Nevis and was orphaned as a young boy. He learned to speak French at an early age and was exposed to the brutality of slavery on the island. He ended up doing accounting work for some wealthy exporters and by age 14, had taken over their businesses' bookkeeping. Recognizing his potential, they sent him to New York to be educated. He enrolled in King's College in Manhattan, New York, at age 16 in 1775. Swept up by anti-British sentiment, he ended up as a junior artillery officer in New York when the British fleet arrived in July 1776. He came to Washington's attention in the Battle of Brooklyn and, again, at Princeton that fall. Brilliant, educated and extremely ambitious, he was destined to do great things and he knew it.

Lafayette, too, suffered loss as a child. His father died heroically fighting for France in the Seven Years War, and the young marquis was in line to inherit his father's estate and pension when he turned 25. He added enormously to his wealth, at age 16, marrying the daughter of Jean de Noailles, Duc d'Ayen, who was well connected in the Royal Court of Louis XVI. His decision in May 1777 to sail to America with Baron DeKalb was impetuous, to say the least, arriving in Philadelphia at a pivotal moment. When he decided to leave Paris, his wife Adrienne was pregnant, and she decided to remain in Paris with her father. By August 1777, Lafayette had a daughter that he had not yet met. Like Hamilton, he was ambitious to a fault but his loyalty to Washington would prove to be his greatest asset.

John Laurens was born into wealth in 1754 and was descended from French Huguenots in South Carolina. His father, Henry Laurens, started an import-export business in Charleston years earlier, and it was enormously successful. One of the products he dealt in was slaves from the Caribbean and Africa. He then expanded and moved into the plantation business north of Charleston, adding to his already enormous wealth. His plantations were spread over 3,000 acres in Monck's Corner on the Cooper River. He married and had twelve children but only four survived into adulthood. John was the oldest of the four. In 1770, Henry's wife died, and he decided to educate his children in Europe. John was enrolled at the University in Paris and studied under such men as Jean-Jacques Rousseau, one of the premier political philosophers of the day. His influence on young John Laurens was significant. John learned to speak French fluently, finished his studies there and then moved to London where he studied law for two years. The events at Lexington and Concord enraged him, and he desired to return and join the fight. He turned 21 in late 1776 and as he read the continued accounts of the conflict in America, he wrote to his father frequently about his desire to join the fight for independence.

Then, a test of his honor occurred. He impregnated a young girl, Matilda Manning, he was seeing in London. He married her early in her pregnancy to protect her honor, sparing her the shame of bearing an illegitimate child. As her pregnancy progressed, he spoke to her frequently about his plans to go to America.

Matilda told him she would make plans to join him in America with their child, but John convinced her to remain behind in her father's house in London. John left for America in December 1776 as Washington was planning to cross the Delaware and surprise the Hessian garrison at Trenton. His father convinced him to stop first in Paris and meet with Ben Franklin, which he did. After that meeting, he wrote to his father that,

"France does not choose to involve herself in a war with England."

[Unger, 35-36]

The return voyage to America was not without incident. They were stopped and searched by a British frigate, but John's papers did not indicate his rebel interests. The British also did not know he was the son of a member of the American Congress.

His daughter, Frances Eleanor Laurens, was born in early 1777. John's wife Matilda tried once again to join him in America, but her father convinced her to stay, pointing out the obvious risks of travel with an infant child. John would write to her frequently in the next few years, but history would intervene.

John Laurens returned to South Carolina just as his father was elected President of the Continental Congress.

These three young men, all fluent in French, found themselves as advisors to George Washington in the fall of 1777. Samuel Huger would be their assistant, documenting their deliberations, delivering highly confidential letters to Washington's field commanders, and proposing ideas to the three aides. Samuel became close to all three, acting as the eyes and ears of what was happening within Washington's rank and file.

They all met for the first time the next day. Despite their incredibly varied backgrounds, they had much in common. They were all very young and highly educated. Lafayette and Laurens were married. They all spoke French. They were all ambitious to a fault. And, most importantly, they all believed deeply in the cause of American independence from England.

They met in a small room that Hamilton already had obtained in the rear of the inn where he was staying, and they all crammed into that small space. The innkeeper had used that room to store sacks of vegetables so it had a sort of sweet, earthy smell. It was lined with shelves containing various cans and jars of preserved fruit. They sat facing each other, and a window facing a rear courtyard let in diminished sunlight.

Samuel started the discussion. He now knew Lafayette well from their trip up from Charleston. He had only met Laurens that one time. Hamilton, however, was an unknown and Hamilton had never met any of them before.

Samuel opened with, "Let's get right to it. The word is that the army is moving out soon, and we need to advise Washington on many items."

Hamilton was the senior aide and made sure the others knew it so he spoke next, "The general and I have decided how we will all work together. I will manage his personal correspondence and decision making. John, using your father's influence, you will handle all communications with Congress. That will flow from Washington and me to you and then from you to Congress and your father as you see fit. Monsieur de Lafayette, you will advise on matters relating to the French, again coming through me."

Huger spoke up, perhaps out of turn, "Washington must act quickly. Our homes are threatened, and our future is in doubt. These British cowards must be stopped, and quickly, before they return to my state."

Hamilton glanced at the others.

"Well, Mr. Huger, you are somewhat of a Palmetto Patriot now, aren't you?"

But he quickly smiled, lightening the mood in the room. Samuel's moniker had been established.

Hamilton spoke for another couple of minutes before ending the meeting. Alexander Hamilton was drawing lines in an effort to maintain his seniority. This is not how things would actually work but he was trying to set boundaries for these other inexperienced aides. For now, it was fine since they all wanted to get along.

As they walked out of the room, Laurens tapped Samuel on the shoulder, "The Palmetto Patriot, eh? I think I like that."

Chapter 13 ~ *Brandywine, September 1777*

Almost immediately, there were huge issues confronting them. British General Howe's fleet was spotted at the tip of New Jersey and was unquestionably headed towards Philadelphia. There was no doubt now.

After defeating Washington at Brooklyn the previous fall, Howe had debated for some time whether to move his forces north up the Hudson River to assist General Burgoyne who was coming down from Canada. That would give the British complete control of the Hudson, effectively cutting off the New England colonies. Howe's logic, however, was that, if he could unseat the American Congress in Philadelphia, the Americans would be without leadership and funding and the war would end. So, he moved his forces south from New York, not north. The result would be Burgoyne's disastrous defeat at Saratoga and Ticonderoga to the young American General Benedict Arnold later that summer.

In early July, Howe decided to get his fleet ready. After multiple mistimed messages back and forth from Lord Germain in London, he would head to Philadelphia. He might even capture or kill Washington in the process. Germain wanted him to march north to support Burgoyne coming down from Canada, but Germain's note never arrived in New York.

Howe could march across New Jersey to Philadelphia and risk engaging the New Jersey militia or send his fleet down the coast and up the Delaware River to the American capital. The fleet would get him there faster and safer, in about eight days, so he spent a month outfitting the 125 ships that would be needed. Men, horses, wagons, cannons, and a wide variety of supporting supply vessels left New York harbor in early August. As they approached the tip of New Jersey, they were spotted. British loyalists then reported that many American militia units were defending the Delaware River, so Howe decided to continue south and come up the Chesapeake Bay. That was when mother nature intervened. The fleet encountered violent storms followed by strong contrary winds. Lightning struck several ships killing sailors and starting fires. The horses had to be thrown overboard to save the supply ships from sinking. The eight-day trip took 32 days. When Howe put his men ashore in Maryland, they needed several days to recover before marching north.

As the reports of Howe's movements flooded in, Hamilton, Lafayette, Laurens, and Samuel Huger continued to meet in Hamilton's cramped office three times each day. At times like this, Hamilton was smooth, polished and never flustered. He spoke in even tones. In his mind, he was clearly the senior aide-de-camp and the others did not challenge him. After each meeting, Samuel would have a large list of to-dos.

"Time is of the essence. We need to figure out exactly what Howe's plan is. Samuel, you will be our eyes and ears. We have scouts and couriers down the Delaware River and Chesapeake Bay, but we need you to gather their intelligence and bring it to us. Washington is moving the entire northern Continental Army here from Morristown and Valley Forge."

They talked some more, often in French, as all three of Washington's new aides were fluent. Samuel could only loosely follow the conversation as his French was not very good.

Samuel rode out and spent the next two days making connections with the American scouts at various confidential drop points south of Philadelphia. The scouts along the Delaware now reported seeing nothing so he moved west, closer to the Chesapeake Bay.

At one contact point, he met with a Maryland militia captain, "Let Washington know, the British came up the Chesapeake, have disembarked at Elkton, Maryland, and are preparing to march north."

"Captain, what would you estimate their troop strength and artillery?"

"Lieutenant, tell Washington there are five, maybe ten thousand redcoats with maybe 100-200 cannon. Strangely, there were very few on horseback and, perhaps, 500 wagons of supplies and munitions. Reports are they are stealing horses from the local citizens."

Samuel sped back to Philadelphia with that alarming news which was quickly fed to Washington.

The American Commander quickly led his forces out of Philadelphia. He wanted to choose the time and place of the encounter instead of trying to set up defensive works in the city. The Continental Congress would evacuate to Lancaster, Pennsylvania.

On September 5, Washington, along with his generals, met with his three young aides five miles south of Philadelphia. Samuel Huger had just arrived with additional intelligence that the British had broken camp and were on the move north. At a place called Chadd's Ford, the two armies faced each other on opposite sides of Brandywine Creek. Washington held the high ground thinking that would give him a clear advantage. It was here, he decided, that the Americans would make their stand.

On September 11, both sides opened fire, with Washington thinking the main body of the British was directly across from him. Once again, as at Brooklyn a year earlier, the British outflanked him. Howe's second in command General Cornwallis, with 3,000 men, circled around Washington, crossing the creek far downstream. As they closed in, the Americans fled in a panic. Laurens, Hamilton and Lafayette, as non-combat aides, were held back but begged Washington for a chance to join the battle and the commander-in-chief reluctantly relented. Each of the three young men rode off in different directions rallying Americans to hold their ground.

Lafayette was quickly shot in the calf but continued to fight. Laurens was shot in the shoulder and his horse was shot out from beneath him. Seeing him fall, Lieutenant Huger swooped in to save him. He shot one Redcoat who approached with bayonet drawn. Samuel then signaled to two other Continentals to drag the young officer from the field. Samuel followed them with British musket balls whizzing overhead.

"It was not his fault Laurens was not killed or wounded," Lafayette commented many years later.

During the battle, a British Major named Ferguson emerged from the woods on horseback along Brandywine Creek. Forty yards away, sat an American general on horseback with his back to the British officer, unaware of his presence. Ferguson was a noted marksman, one of the best in the British Army.

In his report the next day from a field hospital, he recorded, *"The American senior officer was very tall, sitting atop a magnificent white mare. He was not aware of my presence with his back to me. I pointed my pistol and, for a moment, he looked over his shoulder at me. I did not take the shot as it would be undignified to shoot another officer in the back. He rode slowly away."*

Ferguson's moment to alter the course of history passed.

The lifeless American Army retreated to Chester leaving Philadelphia to the conquering Lord Howe.

As Lafayette and Laurens were evacuated by boat to a field hospital, Washington instructed, *"Treat them as if they were my sons."*

From a hospital bed that evening, Lafayette wrote to his wife Adrienne, *"We fought a difficult battle last night and were not the strongest."*

When the dust settled, 700 Americans lay dead in the field and an additional 400 were captured. For an army short on men and morale, it was a crushing defeat.

[Unger, 52]

This would be the last time Washington would expose the Continental Army to superior British forces. He had learned a hard lesson. For the foreseeable future, the American strategy would be to harass the British, wear them down, not take them on in a frontal assault. It would be three years before Washington had the men and equipment he needed to confront them.

Chapter 14 ~ Winter 1777-1778

The year 1778 would prove to be pivotal in the war for American Independence. The year was marked by two very different situations: A stalemate in the north and a new British offensive in the south. And in Paris, a momentous decision was about to be made.

The winter of 1777-1778 was the lowest point thus far for the Continental Army. After the defeat at Brandywine, Washington retreated to winter quarters in Valley Forge, Pennsylvania, some 20 miles from Philadelphia. The British settled comfortably into Philadelphia to wait out the winter. Invoking The Quartering Acts of 1765, the British soldiers occupied nearly every private residence in town, displacing the local citizens.

At Washington's camp, conditions were brutal with one of the coldest winters on record. One quarter of Washington's forces either died from exposure or came down with smallpox. Food was scarce, shelter was primitive.

In February 1778, the Congress, while in exile in Lancaster, Pennsylvania, issued a resolution that Washington and all of his officers be required to sign an oath of allegiance renouncing the King of England. This did not sit well with many of the officers. John Laurens was infuriated when he heard of Congress' decision and went, at once, to see his father. He found him set up temporarily in a Lancaster church that the local pastor has afforded him as his office. The guards admitted John without an appointment and he stormed in without the usual niceties.

"Father, are you and the Congress mad? Do you understand the deprivations that we have suffered in Valley Forge? Now you are bringing into question our officers' loyalty?"

Henry Laurens sat behind a desk with his arms folded across his chest. He let his son go on for several minutes until John finally exhausted his argument and sat down glaring at his father.

"Are you done, son? This oath is merely a formality, one that many European leaders have requested from their military leaders. I think you are overreacting."

They went back and forth for a few more minutes and, by then, several members of Congress were waiting to see John's father. John, still upset, stormed out of the room and rode back to camp.

In the end, the oath was administered without incident and the issue faded. Alexander Hamilton, John Laurens and even the French officer Lafayette all signed it in early May with Lord Stirling, one of Washington's generals, witnessing the signatures. Hamilton famously signed it "Alex." The oath read:

"I, John Laurens, aide-de-camp, do acknowledge the United States of America, to be Free, Independent and Sovereign States, and declare that the people thereof owe no allegiance or obedience to George the Third, King of Great-Britain; and I renounce, refuse and abjure any allegiance and obedience to him; and I do Swear that I will to the utmost of my power, support, maintain and defend the said United States, against the said King George the Third, his heirs and successors and his or their abettors, assistants and adherents, and will serve the said United States as afore'd, which I now hold, with fidelity, according to the best of my skill and understanding."

Stirling signed it, *"Sworn before me, Camp at Valley Forge, May 12th, 1778, Stirling Major General."*

Hamilton, Laurens, Lafayette and Huger met regularly during that winter and the mood was grim. One particularly wintry morning they crowded together in a small hut with a fire in one corner. As the wind howled outside, snow was piled high against the canvas walls. The small fire crackled, casting flickering shadows on the faces of these men sitting around a small table covered in maps and letters.

Hamilton, intense and sharp-eyed, sat straight-backed with quill in hand, furiously writing a letter. He blew into his hand in the hope of circulating the blood to his fingers and occasionally glanced at the flickering flame as if calculating something. Next to him, Lafayette leaned over the maps, his fingers tracing routes and plans. He stretched out his leg, the one that absorbed that British musket shot at Brandywine. Across from them sat John Laurens, his arm still in a sling from Brandywine, reading a report from his father's Congress. The fourth man was Samuel, spinning his quill between his fingers waiting for one of them to speak.

Finally, Hamilton was first to speak, "John, if Congress doesn't send the supplies soon, I don't know how much longer the men can last."

He paused for a beat, dipping his quill into the near frozen inkwell.

"Washington can't perform miracles with nothing."

At moments like this, Lafayette was never at a loss for words. His French accent was still pronounced. He looked up from the map.

"Monsieur Washington is like no other general I have seen. The men, they trust him like un père- … father. But they need more than trust to fight."

John Laurens took this all in. He had been raised in utter wealth and these deprivations were a horror to him. But at times like this, he would get philosophical, recalling the various history lessons he had learned in Paris.

"We're supposed to be the army of a revolution but we look more like beggars. And Washington … he's breaking under the pressure, even if he won't show it."

Hamilton said, "Yes, I've seen it. He spends hours pacing by the fire, refusing to sleep. He knows the responsibility he carries. If we fail, this whole experiment fails."

Hamilton glared at Laurens, blaming him vicariously for the inaction of his father's Congress.

"He's fighting not just the British but the Congress, the governors, everyone is too slow to see the urgency."

Lafayette took this all in,

"In France, we talk of heroes, men like Caesar, Alexander the Great. But Washington ... he is different. He does not want glory. He fights for something larger. He fights for liberty and that is why I came here."

"You came here because you're a stubborn idealist, Lafayette." Laurens smiled, "Like the rest of us."

John Laurens stood up. "Samuel, let's go. If we leave now, we can make it to where Congress is meeting by nightfall and talk to my father. If the American Congress cannot supply us, then my father's fortune will."

Lafayette stood then. "I will write to France again. The king's court must understand how dire our situation is. If Washington can hold on, perhaps we can secure more supplies, more soldiers from King Louis."

Hamilton was the last to stand, signaling that the meeting was over. He picked up his coat, fastening it tightly and pulling it high around his neck.

"Washington has held this army together with his bare hands. We owe him everything. Now it's up to us to make sure he doesn't break under the weight of it all."

These three young men stood in silence for a moment, each lost in their own thoughts, staring at each other. Outside, the cold wind continued to howl, a reminder of the relentless struggle they faced.

But in the modest warmth of the hut, there was an unspoken bond between them—a shared understanding that they were all fighting for something far greater than themselves. It was up to them.

With that, they moved to leave, ready to face the cold and the daunting battles ahead, their loyalty to Washington and each other unshaken.

John and Samuel traveled to meet with John's father and secured personal funds from him for supplies.

In February, John Laurens and Samuel Huger exposed a scandal among the American forces. With men starving, it was learned that Washington's Quartermaster, Thomas Mifflin, was secretly stealing supplies from the army and selling them. Mifflin was a profit-oriented Philadelphia merchant and appointing him Quartermaster was, in hindsight, a foolish move by Washington.

Laurens and Huger had been dispatched to the countryside to purchase supplies with the Huger family funds and saw an American wagon with men they knew were from the Quartermaster's command. They secretly followed the wagon down to the river and watched as the men loaded the food and blankets onto a small barge. Money changed hands and the men returned to the Quartermaster's camp. It was clear what was happening.

The Quartermaster was exposed and court-martialed, and things began to slowly improve. John's father, Henry Laurens, personally spent large sums on provisions for the men and that started to make a difference. Despite the leg wound suffered at Brandywine, Lafayette played a major role in training the Americans that spring and maintaining morale. John Laurens also recovered from his shoulder wound at Brandywine and began to think beyond the current conflict.

Around that time, Lafayette began his campaign of letter writing to France enlisting support for America's fight for independence. He started with his father-in-law, Jean de Noailles, who was high up in the Court of King Louis. Lafayette also wrote to Ben Franklin, now America's lead emissary in Paris. He wrote nearly every day assuming that some letters might not arrive.

Chapter 15 ~ Recognition, May 1778

On May 1, 1778, a rider arrived in the American Morristown, New Jersey camp and breathlessly sprinted to Washington's tent. In late March, urged on by Franklin's lobbying and Lafayette's relentless letter writing, along with the American victory at Saratoga in October, the French began to think differently about America's chances. The British were their hated adversary.

Washington calmly opened the letter while his aides and senior staff stood around him. His eyes glistened.

The French government would now recognize America's independence. In France's eyes, America would be a sovereign state. The reaction by Washington and his staff was electric. Uncharacteristically, the General went around the large command tent hugging everyone, even his negro orderlies.

The British Parliament reacted almost immediately and declared war on France. The die was cast. France would eventually enter the fray on the side of the Americans. Nobody knew what shape that support would eventually take.

The British were deciding on a new strategy and that included replacing Howe in North America. His disastrous decision to abandon Burgoyne on the Hudson was the last straw for Lord Germain in London.

The new British commander, General Clinton, now in charge, took notice. His forces were spread out across New York and Philadelphia. He had to assume a French assault was coming.

Samuel was called to a meeting with Hamilton, Lafayette and Laurens. They huddled in Hamilton's makeshift office in their rooming house. Samuel took out his quill to take notes as was his responsibility. These were the kind of critical discussions that needed to be recorded. These three young aides to Washington shaped the commander-in-chief's decisions.

Hamilton spoke first. "This changes everything. We need to be prepared to meet with the French to decide how to proceed. D'Estaing has been appointed Admiral by the French king and is sure to sail soon."

Laurens spoke next. "I will talk to my father about appointing a liaison from Congress and adding to Franklin's staff in Paris. We need more representation in King Louis' Court. I met with Franklin last year, and he is infirmed and cannot do it alone."

Little did John Laurens know that he would eventually be part of that liaison team in Paris.

Lafayette, ever the military planner, said, "I know d'Estaing well from my time in France. When the time comes, I will go and meet with him. But rest assured, Clinton will react to this news, without a doubt. I suspect he feels exposed in Philadelphia."

Chapter 16 ~ Monmouth Courthouse

Lafayette was right. It was time for Clinton to consolidate forces back in New York in advance of a possible French assault. New York was a more defensible position. In early June 1778, Clinton sent 3,000 men by ship back to New York and led the rest, with all of their equipment, out of Philadelphia on the trek across New Jersey. The baggage train of 1,500 carriages extended for 12 miles.

Reports flooded into Washington's staff. Clinton was abandoning Philadelphia. What was left of the Continental Army left Valley Forge, invigorated at the chance to attack a retreating British column.

Washington and his generals, Charles Lee, Nathanael Greene, and Horatio Gates, met to discuss the situation. With Laurens, Hamilton, Lafayette, and Huger standing off to the side in Washington's tent, a plan was devised.

A week of searing heat, heavy rains and suffocating humidity slowed the British advance to six miles a day. In late June, the British made camp near Monmouth Courthouse in central New Jersey.

Washington rode out with Hamilton, Lafayette and Laurens at the head of the American column.

Washington saw his opportunity. He assigned General Charles Lee, the same general who had been rebuffed in Charleston by Moultrie and Francis Marion two years earlier, to lead the assault. Lee had been ignominiously captured by a British patrol in New Jersey the previous year and was later released.

What nobody knew was that, while imprisoned, Lee, a former British officer, was actively collaborating with Clinton and upon his release, he began providing information to Clinton hoping to unseat Washington.

Washington unwittingly assigned Lee to this command and Lee told Washington that letting the British retreat unabated to New York would put them in a position to negotiate a settlement. He declined to attack, and Washington relieved him in the field in front of all his men. Lee was later charged with insubordination and court martialed.

General Nathanael Greene was then put in charge. The battle commenced.

Lafayette at one point was encircled by a British counterattack and led a column of men *"out of death's jaws"* as he later described it. Laurens, as at Brandywine a year earlier, had his horse shot from beneath him and continued the fight on foot waving his sword wildly in the air. And again, as at Brandywine, it was his fellow South Carolinian Samuel Huger who swept in and scooped him up.

Meanwhile, Alexander Hamilton was assigned by Washington to investigate what was happening and while riding back, also had his horse killed. Hamilton suffered serious injuries, made it back to report to Washington and collapsed in a field hospital tent.

With fresh information and General Greene commanding, Washington personally directed his forces and inflicted enormous casualties on the retreating British column.

"General Washington was never greater in battle than in this action," Lafayette beamed in his memoirs.

It was this day, more than any other, that endeared Hamilton, Lafayette and Laurens to Washington as his *"three sons."*

Night fell and before Washington could seal his victory, Clinton and his troops slipped away in the fog and darkness. He led his column to Sandy Hook, New Jersey, where waiting transports ferried the badly defeated British Army back to New York. More than 1,000 British soldiers had been killed.

Philadelphia and all of New Jersey were now safely controlled by the Americans. The Continental Congress, in exile in York, Pennsylvania, returned to Philadelphia.

Lafayette and Laurens went to see Hamilton in a field hospital tent that evening. He had broken ribs and his shoulder was in a sling. He managed to stand and salute his comrades.

"It was a good day, wasn't it?" he beamed.

"It was a glorious day," gushed Lafayette.

Hamilton quickly recovered and was soon back at Washington's side in the now liberated city of Philadelphia.

That fall, a ball was held in Philadelphia and hosted by the Continental Congress in honor of General Washington. His wife Martha traveled up from Mount Vernon and at the dance, Hamilton met his future wife, Elizabeth Schuyler, the daughter of the New York Governor. Lafayette and Laurens, the two young married men with their wives thousands of miles away, danced with every woman present, as did George Washington. It was a moment to put the reality of war out of their minds for a few hours.

The fall of 1778 marked the beginning of a long stalemate between Washington and Clinton in the northeast that would last for two more years. Each side was convinced it could not prevail over the other.

But the year 1778 was not over and the British "Southern Strategy" was about to commence.

Chapter 17 ~ Newport

On July 5, 1778, shortly after the victory at Monmouth Courthouse, the French fleet was spotted off the coast of Maryland. It was commanded by Charles Henri Hector, known as le Comte d'Estaing, and he brought with him 12 ships of the line, four frigates, and 4,000 French marines. On board the flagship was Conrad Alexandre Gerard, France's first ambassador to America. Silas Deane, America's first French liaison in Paris and who had been replaced by Benjamin Franklin, was also on board. It was Deane who had recklessly issued Continental Army commissions to many French Army officer, and he had been recalled by Congress. Two of those commissions were to Lafayette and Baron DeKalb.

The voyage took 87 days with rough seas and contrary winds. Had the French arrived a few weeks earlier, they could have trapped Clinton in Philadelphia but by July, Clinton was safely back in New York having been bloodied at Monmouth Courthouse a month earlier. A new plan had to be worked out with the French.

After dropping off the diplomatic passengers, d'Estaing anchored off Sandy Hook, New Jersey, on July 17 for meetings with Washington's representatives.

[Duncan, 83-88]

For Lafayette, this is what he had been waiting for. Since arriving in Winyah Bay, North Island, South Carolina, a year earlier, he had privately maintained his desire to rejoin the French military once the American conflict was over.

He wrote to his wife that night, *"My dearest Adrienne, I must tell you of the most wonderful news. Our French Navy has arrived here in America. This is what we have been waiting for. With d'Estaing we can now overcome the British, win America's independence and I can return to you. It won't be long now."*

Lafayette was selected to represent Washington in the discussions with d'Estaing.

The initial plan was a coordinated assault on Clinton in New York. But the French soon discovered a problem. The heavy French warships could not clear the bar at the narrows to enter New York harbor. An enormous fee was offered to any American harbor pilot who could navigate that entrance but none stepped forward.

A second plan was then developed with an assault on Newport, Rhode Island. Newport had been in British hands since the start of the war and was monitored by a small Continental force under General John Sullivan. Washington commissioned Lafayette with 2,000 men and sent him to Newport to bolster Sullivan's strength. John Laurens was designated to sail with d'Estaing aboard his flagship as Washington's liaison, a strong sign of his confidence in the young South Carolinian. John's command of the French language was a major factor in that decision. Hamilton remained in Philadelphia with Washington, and Samuel Huger joined Lafayette as a lieutenant-colonel on the march to Newport.

Lafayette arrived in September with the French already anchored off of Newport and he was quickly taken out to meet with d'Estaing. They had met previously in France before Lafayette's departure. In Washington's mind, Lafayette, as a former French Army officer, was the logical choice for this assignment. Climbing on board the flagship, however, Lafayette was met with icy stares from the French naval officers. He was, after all, in America in violation of King Louis XVI's orders. Was Lafayette a traitor to France?

After a long meeting with the admiral, Lafayette was able to convince him of his continuing loyalty to the French monarch.

Lafayette wrote, *"I have always thought, and I have written and said everywhere, that I would rather be a soldier in the French service than a general officer anywhere else."*

[Duncan, 85]

D'Estaing then offered Lafayette a great opportunity. He would lead a combined French and American command, attacking Newport from one side, while Sullivan attacked from the other. D'Estaing's gunships would bombard the British positions in a coordinated assault.

The American forces on land were also augmented – first, by the arrival of General Nathanael Greene, and then, by John Hancock, politician turned field commander. Everything appeared to favor the Americans.

Sullivan, Greene, Hancock, and Lafayette met to discuss tactics and logistics. The meeting got off on the wrong foot.

Sullivan glared at Lafayette.

"Sir, you have given away our leadership in this assault to your countrymen, I suspect, to curry favor with your king. The men you command, assigned to you by Washington, are American boys fighting for America. We don't give a damn about the two-hundred-year-old squabble between your king and King George."

Greene and Hancock nodded in agreement. Hancock said, "This is an American operation with French naval offshore support. When this is over, the American flag will fly over Newport, not France's."

Sullivan, at one point, refused to allow Lafayette to detach himself and lead the French troops as d'Estaing had suggested. For two days they argued.

Sullivan then launched his forces hours ahead of schedule. In his mind, the French were here to assist him. The French on board the flagship were aghast at this breach of honor.

John Laurens watched with disgust from his position as American liaison on d' Estaing's flagship. Their wounded pride was all the French seemed to care about. European wars evidently involved a certain protocol and were conducted as a matter of honor.

The French admiral then refocused on the mission. Affronts could be settled later. He launched his 4,000 marines on the original schedule as the British retreated within the walls of Newport.

Things then went sideways. British sails were spotted on the horizon and d'Estaing had a decision to make. Abandon the assault and deal with the approaching British Navy or ignore them and focus on Newport. He left behind a few French frigates in support of Sullivan and sailed out to meet the British.

On August 11, nature stepped in and an enormous storm arrived, battering both fleets. The storm raged for 72 hours with extremely high winds. The French fleet was not heard from for several days, pushed well out to sea. The storm passed and, finally, on August 20, d'Estaing limped back into view. One French warship was lost, many more damaged. The admiral's flagship itself was demasted and had to be towed back to Newport. The admiral quickly decided his fleet must withdraw and go to Boston for repairs.

The British Navy, also heavily damaged, had withdrawn back to New York.

Lafayette and Sullivan had another very public disagreement with Sullivan, irate that the French had abandoned the fight, and Lafayette, defending his countrymen. It was then agreed by all to abandon the attack on Newport.

Lafayette traveled to Boston to repair the relationship with d'Estaing, and Sullivan withdrew, now outnumbered by the British in Newport four to one.

Soon after, one hundred more British ships arrived in Newport, sent by Clinton from New York. Had d'Estaing remained in Newport, his damaged fleet would have been decimated and French naval support for America would cease to exist. The outcome of the American Revolution would have been vastly different.

As fall turned to winter in 1778 and Washington made plans to camp at Valley Forge, Washington ordered Lafayette to return to France to assist Franklin. The original plan was for Lafayette to accompany d'Estaing back to France but the French admiral decided to winter in the Caribbean once his repairs in Boston were done. Positioning that fleet in those waters would prove beneficial to Washington in 1779 and 1780.

Samuel Huger, John Laurens, and Lafayette met in late December in Boston. It was not clear if they would ever see each other again.

"Mes amis, you have become my closest friends in America. I would not be here today if not for you."

His English was improving.

The two young South Carolinians looked across the table at this still-boyish looking Frenchman. He now seemed older than his years and his bravery on the battlefield had been evident at Brandywine. Washington had grown very fond of him. Lafayette, however, was smarting from his failures at Newport.

"Marquis, it has been an honor serving with you," Laurens offered, trying to stem his emotions.

Lafayette then looked at Samuel.

"And you, monsieur Huger, you have been with me from the beginning, when I first set foot in America, to this very moment. Our friendship will be eternal and I will always cherish our campfire discussions on our trip to Philadelphia from Charleston two years ago."

They all stood, saluted each other, and then hugged.

John and Samuel returned to Valley Forge with Washington and on January 11, 1779, the Marquis de Lafayette boarded the *Alliance* in Boston as it set sail from Boston. He would join Franklin at the Court of King Louis XVI to plead Washington's cause.

He was also going home to his wife and child. But he was determined to return.

Chapter 18 ~ The Southern Strategy, 1779

In the fall of 1778, 3,000 miles away in London, a meeting was held. Lord Germain, the British minister for American affairs, conferred with King George and his military planners. Despite the victory at Brandywine and the occupation of Philadelphia in 1777, the disaster at Monmouth Courthouse that summer made it into the British press. The pressure to defeat these damned Americans was increasing. More importantly, the French were now coming into the conflict. It seemed the war in America was at a stalemate. The British Treasury was feeling the effects of supporting hundreds of ships and arming tens of thousands of soldiers 3,000 miles away.

The meeting with King George was to discuss "*the American situation.*" The King had many things on his mind and, to be honest, this conflict with the colonies was not high on his list. Germain did all the talking. He had a proposal.

"Your highness, New York City is firmly in British hands and our Navy remains unchallenged. Washington has eluded being killed or captured but he is trapped. Our new field commander, Henry Clinton, is ready to act. I am proposing a completely new strategy. Take the American south. We can easily establish a foothold with Savannah and the Georgia countryside is mostly loyalist. We move next and take Charleston, cutting off their economy. We recruit the many thousands of black slaves in South Carolina to fight with us, with a promise of emancipation. We occupy South Carolina and move north through North Carolina and Virginia, again gaining loyalist and negro support along the way. We put Washington in a vise. His army is already nearly shattered, and he will lose popular support. This will all be over in a year."

It was Germain's brainchild and called, "*The Southern Strategy.*" British forces would be divided with most of the fleet and troops sent south. First to Georgia, which was the colony most sympathetic to British rule. Savannah would be reinforced, then Charleston, the richest town in America. Loyalists from Georgia and South Carolina were expected to arise, and thousands of black slaves would join with British forces to sweep north through North Carolina and Virginia burning and pillaging everything in its path. It would force Washington into a confrontation and put him in a vise from which he would be forced to sue for peace.

At least, that was the plan.

Chapter 18 ~ Clinton Arrives

With the failed attempt at Fort Sullivan in Charleston harbor of 1776 still fresh in his mind and new supplies on its way from London, Clinton accepted the *Southern Strategy* from Lord Germain as his own and put the plan in place. He was anxious to redeem himself after Monmouth.

But it took many months to prepare, and the supplies from London were slow in coming. Moving an entire army nearly 1,000 miles by ship from New York to South Carolina was an enormous planning challenge. It was decided that 90 troopships, carrying 13,500 men, 1,500 horses, cannons, munitions, wagons, supplies, and everything needed for a military expedition, were required. This would start out as a naval assault in Charleston and then a ground operation through South Carolina, North Carolina, and Virginia. Clinton would personally lead the initial assault and then turn the ground operation over to Cornwallis, his most trusted and experienced field commander.

General Cornwallis would be the battlefield commander in the south. He was ruthless and had an even more savage commander, Major Banastre Tarleton, under his command. Tarleton had distinguished himself at Brooklyn and later across New Jersey. It was Tarleton who had famously captured American General Lee in his nightclothes in New Jersey the previous year.

Charleston was the fourth largest American city after Boston, Philadelphia, and New York. It was also the richest. Fueled by the global rice and indigo trade, profitable plantations abounded up and down the rivers that led to Charleston. They were owned by several members of the American Congress. The largest and most profitable belonged to Henry Laurens, the President of the Congress.

Charleston traded with the world and its waterfront was littered with trading vessels of all shapes and sizes. Charleston shops offered fine products from every country. British, French, Portuguese, Russian, Spanish and even Chinese goods lined the shops' shelves which the wealthy plantation owners eagerly purchased. Even with the British war going on, trade was brisk. Most of the armaments and ammunition now fueling the war effort also flowed through Charleston, much of it via smugglers.

In King George's mind, taking Charleston would suffocate the American cause.

Chapter 20 ~ South Carolina, 1778-1779

Francis Marion had a problem. It had been two years since he assumed command of the 2nd Regiment of the South Carolina Continental Army, and there had been virtually no fighting with the British. General Clinton had left the south in 1776 after his disastrous effort to take Fort Sullivan (now called Fort Moultrie) at the mouth of Charleston harbor, and it was not known when, or if, the British would return.

Word of American victories at places like Monmouth Court-house in New Jersey and Saratoga in New York bolstered American optimism in the south. Perhaps the war would end in the north with no more death and destruction in the Carolinas and Georgia.

But Savannah seemed vulnerable with only a small, inexperienced American garrison to defend it. Lord Germain in London was planning to bring the war to Marion's doorstep but Marion had no way of knowing that. His only action in the last year was suppressing civil war in the South Carolina upstate between French Huguenots and Presbyterians.

Marion, despite being only 5' 2" tall, was an officer who demanded decorum and discipline from his troops, but the idleness of the last year was working against him. In the absence of a serious imminent threat, he felt his men had become lax and undisciplined. He court-martialed nearly 20% of his command for their inappropriate behavior and violation of his many rules and, as a result, many men had deserted or let their term of service expire.

His command was authorized at 300 but by the fall of 1778, he was at half strength.

It had been a very difficult time for him personally, as well. Born in 1734, the same year as George Washington, he was premature at birth. By far the smallest of five Marion boys and the *"runt of the litter,"* as his father had called him, he was always struggling to keep up. His older brothers all married wealthy plantation heiresses in the 1760s and as a young man, Francis went his own way. He signed on with a ship's crew, was shipwrecked in the Caribbean and one of only a handful to survive. He then tried his hand at farming on plantation property owned by one his brothers, Belle Isle, near Georgetown. To his surprise, he was a successful farmer and, at nearly forty years old, had resigned himself to that life. He walked with a limp, another side effect of a childhood disease. He was not an attractive man and had never married.

One of his brothers convinced him in 1774 to run with him for the South Carolina legislature, and they both won seats. Military assignments came to him almost by accident as he was assigned a small militia unit out of Georgetown. When word of Bunker Hill and Lexington made its way to South Carolina in 1776, men like Marion could only wonder what the impact would be on them. Then the British showed up at Fort Sullivan in 1776 and Marion's military leadership was on full display. He distinguished himself in front of General Moultrie and was promoted. The British left Charleston in defeat and things quieted down in South Carolina.

By late 1778, Marion had lost three of his four brothers to various diseases, and he was surrogate father to several of his nephews. Four of them were now junior officers in his militia regiment.

After the attack on Fort Moultrie, Marion had been promised a future promotion to Brigadier General but without additional battlefield performances to add to his resume, his commanding officer, General Moultrie, could not make the case to Washington some 700 miles away in New Jersey.

Then in October 1778 word was received that a British force was converging on Savannah. Marion's long period of inactivity was over. The British were back in the South.

Chapter 21 ~ Savannah

The British *Southern Strategy* would start in Georgia by taking Savannah, the second most important southern city. As Clinton in New York was getting his new orders from London, a British general named Prevost, without orders, came up from Florida with a small force and impatiently began an assault on Savannah. He was hoping to retire soon and wanted one more victory to add to his resume. He was not about to wait for some long-term strategy from London and let Clinton upstage him.

Georgia was the colony believed to be the most loyal to King George. On December 29, 1778, a modest British fleet positioned itself along the Savannah waterfront and the mayor surrendered with hardly a shot fired. The 800 members of his small Continental garrison were now prisoners of war. Loyalists from the Georgia countryside poured into the city plundering rebel homes and businesses.

Washington was dismayed to hear of yet another setback – Brooklyn, Brandywine, Newport, and now Savannah. But his resources were stretched very thin, and he was limited in what he could do. The winters at Valley Forge had been severe and none of his troops was in a condition to march nearly 800 miles and fight. He had one Continental commanding officer, Benjamin Lincoln, with around 6,000 troops in South Carolina but they were poorly equipped, ill fed, and largely untested. There were also militia groups scattered around the state but poorly organized under

General Moultrie. One of those groups was Francis Marion's. Lincoln and Moultrie both desperately needed supplies and reinforcements.

It was obvious what Clinton's next target would be after Savannah – Charleston. In the spring of 1779, General Moultrie positioned his regiments there, including Francis Marion's 2nd Regiment.

As spring turned to summer in 1779, it seemed only a matter of time before Charleston would come under attack.

Chapter 22 ~ Manumission

In the late summer of 1778, John Laurens called a meeting in Philadelphia with Hamilton and Lafayette. Samuel Huger, as per their daily custom, was in attendance to record. John opened the discussion saying, "I have an idea to discuss with you."

These three young advisors to Washington had quickly bonded, and it had become their norm to try out new ideas in front of each other. Much of it involved grandiose schemes and strategies that never amounted to anything.

"Samuel and I have been discussing a proposal that we would like you to consider. We have a large untapped force at our disposal to assist in fighting the British. It is our slaves. We have tens of thousands of them across our 13 colonies. They are strong, capable and, for the most part, opposed to the British. I think we should assemble some black regiments, prepare them for battle and offer them freedom and compensation at the end of the war."

John looked around the room to read Hamilton and Lafayette's faces. Slavery was the unspoken dichotomy of the American fight for independence and freedom. After all, the Declaration of Independence included the phrase "*all men are created free.*" The irony of his proposal was that the majority of the Laurens' family wealth was derived from the slave trade. John's father, Henry, had been the largest slave trader in the South prior to the war. John's proposal was directly challenging his own family's livelihood.

John Laurens, in his years studying in France and England, had developed strong feelings about slavery. His family, however, operated eight plantations in South Carolina and Georgia, utilizing the labor of hundreds of slaves. Hamilton, Lafayette, and Laurens had discussed the subject previously over dinner but now there was a proposal on the table. Hamilton, always the one more circumspect, held back, allowing Lafayette to speak.

"America's tolerance of enslaving another man has always intrigued me. The first men I met when I came to your shores were negro slaves. We have servants in France but even they have certain rights. Here, your slaves are property with no rights. In France, men and women are … how do you say it? …

Laurens interrupted and finished the sentence, "Indentured."

"Ah, yes, indentured. They are contracted for a period of time to work off debt or lineage or a crime. But never owned. I do not pretend to fully understand the complexity of implementing John's idea here but I think it is something we should pursue."

Lafayette's English was definitely improving, and he was proud of his ability to articulate that argument.

Hamilton thought first of the politics of the situation as he always did. How would Washington react? Would arming slaves open the colonies up to insurrection? What would Congress do? Certainly, the southern states would oppose the idea.

"I think it is worth a discussion with the General. Keep in mind, his family owns many slaves in Virginia, and I suspect he will not be enthusiastic about the idea."

They agreed to take the idea forward. Samuel would draft the proposal, John would review it and present it first to Washington, then to his father and, hopefully, to Congress. It would take several months into 1779 to get all this done but Samuel and John were committed.

A week later, they held a private meeting with Washington in his quarters with John's father in attendance. Samuel kept stealing glances back and forth at the two leaders, trying to read their reaction. Henry Laurens was clearly not in support. Washington was much harder to read.

When John Laurens finished pleading his case, he sat down. For a long moment, there was silence in the room until Washington finally spoke.

"The idea has merit, and I think we should pursue it. Henry, you will have to canvass your colleagues. Gilbert, I would like you to think about military training and assigning officers. "

Nobody knew it then but, in his will, Washington had directed that all the slaves on his Mt. Vernon plantation be emancipated upon his death. Henry Laurens, the President of the Continental Congress, was understandably more circumspect. Being a southern plantation owner, he thought deeper about the politics and economics of it. But after some more discussion, he agreed to take it to certain Congressmen privately. More men were needed in the fight against the British. Samuel and John drafted up a bill for Congress.

Chapter 23 ~ Returning Home

With the fall of Savannah and their home state threatened, Samuel Huger and John Laurens decided to meet with Washington in the early spring of 1779, seeking permission to return home and join General Moultrie's forces to defend Charleston. It was a difficult decision to leave but this was personal for them. Their families and homesteads were at risk. With Savannah in British hands, South Carolina seemed very vulnerable.

With Lafayette now in France, they told Hamilton of their intentions and then made their formal request, in writing, to Washington. He sent for them to meet with him.

The General seemed to have aged in just the short time they had been working together. Deep lines now ran away from his eyes. He rarely smiled, self-conscious about his teeth, but now he looked almost sad. Every time there was a minor success, it seemed to be quickly followed by a crisis or disaster. The joy of the French decision the previous May was followed by months of inaction, the failure in Newport, and now the fall of Savannah, with the expected assault on Charleston. Washington was spending another winter at Valley Forge, and it was more brutal than the first.

He held the letter from his two young aides in his hand and read it aloud back to them.

After a long pause he said, "I understand. I would do the same thing myself. I have come to appreciate you young men but I see your calling to your homeland. I reluctantly agree to your request."

Washington was a man of few words. He wrote out a note to General Lincoln.

"I am assigning you to General Lincoln's command. He has already left for Savannah but you can catch up with him in a few days. God speed."

With that, he stood and extended his hand to the two men who had served him so loyally for the past two years. He handed them the order, and they left camp in late February, stopping in Philadelphia to make their case to Congress for arming slaves.

Laurens' speech, written by Samuel Huger, was powerful. With his father, Henry Laurens, looking on, he closed by saying,

"We Americans in the Southern Colonies cannot contend for liberty until we have enfranchised our slaves."

The proposal called for arming 3,000 slaves in each colony and paying them $50 each at the conclusion of the war.

[Unger, 87]

With Washington's support and to everyone's surprise, the proposal passed. Not wishing to oppose Washington, the Southern States voted for it and then almost immediately weakened it on the grounds that each state had the sole authority to implement it. There was no Federal Government authority at that point to enforce it.

In the end, only Rhode Island would actually field a regiment of all black soldiers.

At this same time, Henry Clinton made known his own offer to the American slaves. Known as the Philipsburg Proclamation, it offered slaves the possibility of freedom if they would take up arms with the British against their American masters.

WHEREAS the Enemy have adopted a practice of enrolling

NEGROES

among their Troops; I do hereby give Notice, That all N E G R O E S taken in Arms, or upon any military Duty, shall be purchased for a stated Price; the Money to be paid to the Captors.

But I do most strictly forbid any Person to sell or claim Right over any N E G R O E, the Property of a Rebel, who may take Refuge with any Part of this Army: And I do promise to every

N E G R O E

Who shall desert the Rebel Standard, full Security to follow within these Lines, any Occupation which he shall think proper.

Given under my Hand at Head-Quarters, PHILIPSBURGH, the 30th Day of JUNE, 1779.

H. CLINTON.

By his Excellency's Command,
JOHN SMITH, Secretary.

The Philipsburg Proclamation of 1779

Chapter 24 ~ The Siege of Savannah

The year 1779 was marked by a series of small British movements in New York, Connecticut, and in the Chesapeake Bay, all designed to draw Washington's forces out into the open. But Washington would not take the bait. Word from France was that Franklin and Lafayette were making progress so Washington was buying time. Despite the fall of Savannah and the near disaster at Newport the previous October, the French fleet under d'Estaing had been repaired and moved to the Caribbean awaiting orders from Paris.

In the summer of 1779, as Clinton and Cornwallis prepared in New York to execute the initial steps of the Southern Strategy, the Americans came up with a plan of their own. They would take Savannah back from the British.

General Benjamin Lincoln, the newly appointed commander of American southern forces, had arrived but now had only had 3,000 inexperienced men under his command. Many Continentals had let their term of service expire, some had even defected and his remaining force was largely untested. Laurens and Huger had recently arrived and were given commands. Washington had also sent a Polish Commander named Casimir Pulaski, who had distinguished himself at Monmouth the year before.

In September, a small French fleet commanded by Admiral d'Estaing arrived in Savannah from the Caribbean. They had now repaired and recovered from the disaster at Newport and were ready to fight. He brought 14 warships and, more importantly,

4,000 troops with him, including 500 men who been conscripted from the island of Santo Domingo and another 500 free blacks from Haiti. This would be the first time that French military forces would engage the British on land in defense of America.

Lincoln also sent word to Francis Marion outside of Charleston to be ready to march with his 300 men at a moment's notice. The French Admiral d'Estaing landed his soldiers outside of the city. This would be a joint attack by American and French forces.

Marion was dispatched and soon arrived in Savannah with Major Peter Horry. This was as distinguished an officer group as the Americans could muster. Surely, they would accomplish their objective and retake Savannah.

A meeting was held with Lincoln, Laurens, d'Estaing, Horry, and Marion with Samuel Huger in the background as an observer. It was clear to Samuel that d'Estaing felt he was in charge and the senior officers quarreled. It was not clear that they agreed on a plan.

In mid-September, d'Estaing, without conferring with Lincoln, sent word to the British Commander of Savannah, General Prevost, to *"yield to the arms of the King of France."*

 Stalling for time, Prevost built a series of square, defensive fortifications around the city called "redoubts" surrounded by ditches and thorny trees with sharpened points. This was a classic European siege defense strategy and not the last time that Americans would face it.

On October 3, the French began bombarding the British with 16-pound cannons from their warships. The British held firm, but time was running out. Hurricane season was approaching, and the French were running out of food on their ships. An outbreak of scurvy then occurred aboard the ships. D'Estaing put an ultimatum to Lincoln, storm the town or abandon the siege. He could wait no longer.

On October 9, in an early morning fog, the Americans attacked.

The battle lasted just one hour and it was a bloodbath. In that hour was the greatest loss of life in the American Revolution since Bunker Hill. A French deserter had informed the British of the American's attack plan, and they were ready.

Multiple assaults were repelled, first by the French, who wanted the "*honor of the vanguard*," then Marion, then Laurens. Marion's standard bearer was cut down and passed the blue flag with a crescent moon to a second man who was also shot and killed.

In that first assault, 500 French soldiers were killed. Of the 600 South Carolinians who charged up the hill to those redoubts in the second wave, 250 did not return. Count Pulaski was cut down by British cannon fire. Laurens exposed himself time and time again but escaped unharmed. French Admiral d'Estaing himself was wounded. A British officer wrote in his journal that night, "*the ditch was choke full of their dead*."

British losses were put at 100-150.

D'Estaing had had enough. He called off the assault and sailed back to France where, years later, he faced the guillotine.

Lincoln gathered what was left of his forces and retreated to Charleston with Savannah now firmly in British hands. He left Marion behind on a plantation outside of Beaufort to monitor the British General Prevost's actions.

The Siege of Savannah was another British victory. All of South Carolina braced for what would come next.

Chapter 25 ~ Charleston, 1780

After many months of delay, Henry Clinton finally left New York, sailing with his fleet the day after Christmas 1779. He arrived five weeks later and anchored in the Savannah River on February 1, with 90 warships and 13,500 men. The American attempt to retake Savannah had failed miserably, and Charleston was now in Clinton's crosshairs. He had spent the winter of 1779-1780 planning the assault.

Washington's aides had been torn apart. Lafayette had now been in France with Franklin for nearly a year. John Laurens and Samuel Huger were in South Carolina with Lincoln and Moultrie after the unsuccessful siege at Savannah. Hamilton remained in Pennsylvania with Washington. They would all write to each other frequently but much of their correspondence never made it.

Colonel John Laurens and Second Lieutenant Samuel Huger had met Lieutenant-Colonel Francis Marion during the Savannah siege and neither was impressed with the other. There was no animosity between them but, then again, not much respect. Samuel and Marion, however, would have a future together.

In early March, both Laurens and Huger took a day to visit their family plantations just outside of the city. It was a chilly ride for Samuel up the coast to Georgetown and out to North Island.

Hostilities had ceased for the moment with both sides awaiting warmer spring weather. Samuel took the ferry out to the Huger plantation in his Continental uniform. So much had changed in the nearly two years that he had been gone. His father came running down the steps with a huge smile on his face to greet his oldest son.

He hugged Samuel like had never done before.

"It is so good to see you, son. Your letters arrive here in batches and I must say, I am impressed at how you have found your way into Washington's company."

"Father, he is an incredible man and a great leader. But we are in trouble. The French have said they recognize us as a sovereign nation but unless we can convince them to supply us with arms and ships, we will not prevail. Savannah has fallen and Clinton is at our doorstep here in Charleston."

Samuel reached for the pitcher of water sitting on the table between them. "You know what they call me in Philadelphia?"

His father turned, his palms upward.

"The Palmetto Patriot. Hamilton thinks I am bit too brash at times."

With that Benjamin Huger beamed.

They talked about the war, the Huger plantation business and life in Philadelphia. Benjamin Huger was now a full Colonel in the local Charleston militia, and his unit was to be stationed behind the lines in the coming siege. He was beginning to send all his slaves back home to their Goose Creek plantation and was planning to shut down the North Island operation near Georgetown.

Samuel asked his father about Rebecca Allston, but his father had not seen or heard anything from her.

Samuel made it a point to go over to the slaves' quarters to greet the many young black men who he had grown up with. He had forgotten how difficult their plantation lives were. They were happy to see him, and he told them about the proposal in front of Congress to arm a black regiment. Their reaction was mixed, untrusting of white laws and legislatures. They had also heard about the British offer in the Phillipsburg Proclamation requiring them to fight on the side of the British. To be honest, they did not trust either side.

Samuel then returned to the main house and had lunch with his father but soon stood up and said abruptly, "Father, I must go now. Lincoln is preparing for the assault and John Laurens and I will be involved in the fight. We don't have much time. Wish me well. Please be careful, yourself, in your assignment. We will see each other again when this is all over."

It was the classic father-son reversal of roles that happens in all families. The son stepping up to take on responsibility.

That was the last conversation they would ever have but, surprisingly, it was not the young South Carolina Continental soldier who would soon meet his maker.

Samuel went over to the Allston plantation home and, once again, arrived unannounced.

It was late afternoon and Rebecca was sitting inside by a fireplace on this chilly afternoon. She and Samuel had corresponded frequently in the last two years but suddenly the letters from her had stopped arriving.

Rebecca, however, was not alone. Sitting with her on the couch was a young South Carolina militia officer whom Samuel did not know. Now 20 years old, she looked more radiant than ever but this officer was clearly the reason her letters had stopped arriving.

They had a brief, awkward conversation but it was obvious to Samuel what had happened. He shook hands with this young militia officer and said goodbye to Rebecca. He was sad and hurt by the experience but knew more important matters were ahead. He returned to the Huger plantation.

Samuel took one of his father's horses and set out for Charleston. He arrived and quickly found John Laurens who was in command of a small regiment on the banks of the Ashley River. If Clinton's men tried to land troops via longboats, it was Laurens' men who were tasked with stopping them. In expectation of a cannon assault from the other side of the river, the men were digging in.

Chapter 26 ~ Lafayette Returns

As Charleston was bracing for the Clinton assault, a ship from France arrived in Boston harbor on April 27, 1780. The passenger on board was the Marquis de Lafayette. He has spent the last 14 months in France living with his wife Adrienne and child, Anastasie, and working with Benjamin Franklin at the Court of Louis XVI. Initially, his arrival back in Paris was filled with tension since he was, technically, a fugitive, having disobeyed the king's direct order against joining the American military. Displaying his diplomatic prowess along with Franklin's support, he was eventually accepted by the king. In fact, the king immediately took a liking to this young Frenchman whose exploits with Washington in America were well documented in Paris. Most of 1779 had been spent with Franklin articulating the American cause.

Lafayette believed he would receive the honor of leading a French force to America. But that honor would fall to another more experienced French general.

Le Comte de Rochambeau was a 54-year-old career French officer who had years of experience fighting the British in The Seven Years War.

King Louis and his foreign minister Vergennes had initially thought of an expedition to the south of England but cancelled it due to winter weather. Slowly, a plan to send the fleet to America evolved.

In hindsight, it was preposterous that this young, relatively junior, officer be given a command of this magnitude but Lafayette's ego permitted him to see himself in that role. When it was made clear that Rochambeau had the appointment, Lafayette acceded and began preparations to return to America to inform Washington.

There was, however, a serious personal matter. His wife Adrienne, who had stood by him all the time he had been gone, was pregnant again. She had begun to think they could live the life of a well-to-do family in Paris with her celebrity husband, who was now a regular in the Court of Louis XVI.

He told her of his plans in early March and she immediately raged at him. She soon cooled off and, with the support of her parents, resigned herself to his decision. When he left, she took to her bed for two weeks.

Upon arrival in Boston, Lafayette was hailed as a hero and several dinners were arranged in his honor. But he had urgent business in Philadelphia. He carried the news that Rochambeau was arriving with 6,000 men and vast amounts of supplies and arms for the Continental Army.

Washington was ecstatic once again at this news and watching for the sails of the French fleet became a daily activity all along the east coast.

Chapter 27 ~ The Siege of Charleston

In April 1780, the good news of the impending arrival of the French fleet and army in the north was tempered by the news from South Carolina.

The British fleet had been at anchor in Savannah all winter. As the spring weather began to warm the south, Clinton approached Sullivan's Island, now named Fort Moultrie, as he had in 1776. This time, however, in the face of overwhelming British firepower, it was quickly abandoned. General Moultrie would have to face the British in Charleston city.

Samuel Huger was busy working with John Laurens on their Ashley River fortifications. They did not know how much time they had but it seemed likely the British might come across at that point to attack Charleston from land.

One day, a rider came up to Laurens stating that he had an urgent message for Lieutenant Huger. An envelope was passed to Samuel and he sat on a log along the river and opened it. It was from his Uncle Isaac Huger, his father's brother, a general under Benjamin Lincoln.

"Samuel, I am sorry to have to tell you that your father Benjamin has lost his life in defense of our country. There are not a lot of details but he was inspecting Charleston's defenses when he was killed. I will arrange for his body to be brought back to our Goose Creek home for interment. I know you are busy preparing our defenses so please

focus on the matter at hand and we will mourn your father together when all this is behind us. Please take care and God bless our country.

Gen. Isaac Huger."

Samuel dropped to his knees and his eyes welled up. His father had always been the rock of the family.

The story emerged slowly, in pieces. Colonel Benjamin Huger, in command of a South Carolina militia battery, went out at dusk to inspect some Charleston fortifications. With the British a few miles away, the local sentries were on edge and one saw Colonel Huger's silhouette on a high wall. Thinking it was a British intruder, he took a shot and killed Samuel's father instantly. Friendly fire. That terrible, illogical expression.

Samuel threw himself into his work the next morning but images of his father, his broad shoulders and strong hands, were etched in his mind. John Laurens did his best to console him. They talked about family long into the night that night, sharing a bottle of rum.

Cornwallis' troops had landed to the south of the city in late March with a strategy of cutting off the city from the rest of South Carolina. He then dispatched the notorious Lieutenant-Colonel Banastre Tarleton to take Moncks Corner, upriver from the city. By early April 1780, the city of Charleston was completely surrounded.

Clinton, from his flagship in the harbor, sent a note to the mayor demanding surrender. No response came back so the British fleet opened fire and soon major parts of Charleston lay in rubble. One of the casualties of the bombardment was the Laurens' mansion, downtown along the waterfront. Knowing that its owner was President of the Continental Congress, the British gunners made it a primary target.

Negotiations began with John Rutledge, South Carolina's Governor. Proposals and counter proposals went back and forth. The British wanted Charleston intact, and Rutledge convinced them to hold off their bombardment until an agreement was reached. He then proposed to surrender the city but that it be allowed to remain neutral and continue its normal economic activity. Clinton originally agreed but then decided against it. Clinton used this extra time to move Cornwallis' men south to Daniel's Island and come up the Ashley River burning plantations along the way.

Clinton finally ran out of patience, and the assault resumed with cannonballs raining down on the city. The British resorted to "heated shot," firing red hot cannon shells, which started fires all over the city.

Rutledge escaped the city on April 13 and headed north. On his way out, he appointed Thomas Sumter as commander of the South Carolina militia. Sumter and Rutledge were neighbors and plantation owners before the war, and the appointment was not well received by the rank and file. Marion was much more deserving.

Marion, like all of the South Carolina militia, was bracing for the attack. But he was incredulous when he was invited to a dinner party in Charleston at the home of one of the wealthier families. Seemingly oblivious to the events around them, they wined and dined their guests and Marion decided to leave early. He excused himself, went upstairs and jumped out a second-floor window, breaking his ankle. He limped to his waiting horse and rode out of town to join his men. He was forced to spend the next month recovering north of the city while major events unfolded.

Samuel and John Laurens' command was along the Ashley River near Middleton Plantation opposite Cornwallis' forces. By April 21, they were dug in with 250 men. Cornwallis' men began to shell them from the other side and then started across the river in small rafts.

Laurens once again decided to put himself in personal danger.

"Samuel, hold this position and I will go down with 50 men and cut them down in the middle of the river as they are crossing. "

It was a good plan but fifty men were not nearly enough. Cornwallis started across the river with hundreds of men in dozens of rafts. Laurens' sharpshooters killed several of them but the Redcoat numbers overwhelmed him.

After both sides had spent their musket ammunition, there was hand to hand fighting at the shoreline and the last that Samuel saw of his commanding officer was him swinging his sword amid five or six Redcoats.

Samuel organized a retreat bringing about 75 men with him. He lost track of where the rest of the unit was. As darkness fell, he managed to move upriver, away from Charleston, as Cornwallis turned downriver towards the city.

Charleston fell on May 12 with much of the city still on fire. General Lincoln proposed to Cornwallis terms of surrender, asking to fly his colors with honor as his Continentals marched out. Cornwallis denied this and what was left of the Continental Army raggedly came out, stacked their weapons and became prisoners of war. Ninety-two Continental soldiers had died with 148 wounded. No count of the civilian deaths was performed. Over five thousand Continentals became British prisoners, 311 American cannons were seized, and around 6,000 muskets were taken. It was the single biggest surrender of men and equipment in the entire war, to that point.

John Laurens was one of the Continentals taken prisoner and it wasn't long before Cornwallis realized, through an informer, that he had this 'high value prisoner,' son of the American President of Congress.

Clinton set up his headquarters in the Motte mansion in Charleston and Cornwallis' men enjoyed the fruits of their victory, ransacking the city. Before long they would move out across South Carolina, expecting little or no resistance in the upstate. Cornwallis let them have their fun in Charleston.

In June, Clinton sailed back to New York leaving Cornwallis with orders to *"clean up South Carolina and move north."*

With the fall of Charleston, all organized government in South Carolina disappeared. Governor John Rutledge left for Philadelphia to beg for assistance and the state legislature ceased meeting.

There was really no organized American resistance remaining in the south except for one man – Francis Marion and his motley crew of freedom fighters. But he was in Georgetown and out of action, nursing his broken ankle.

Samuel Huger assumed command of Laurens' surviving troops and brought them to Marion, who had watched the Charleston disaster from Georgetown. Samuel rode into Marion's camp late one day as Marion leaned on a crutch watching this Continental officer dismount. They had met briefly at Savannah and Marion remembered him.

"Sir, we are at your disposal. Our commanding officer is captured."

Marion looked at this young, disheveled lieutenant, a fellow South Carolinian.

"You are a Huger, are you not, Lieutenant? I know your family well."

He thought for a moment. Samuel did not know Marion very well but he knew the family was from Belle Island plantation.

"Take your place in my South Carolina 2nd Regiment as a first lieutenant. Welcome home, Lieutenant Huger. We are bloodied but not beaten. Cornwallis will rue the day he set foot in South Carolina."

1779 and 1780 were believed, by the British, to be the turning point in the war. The *Southern Strategy* was clearly successful with Savannah and Charleston solidly under British control. There was no apparent American resistance to deal with.

Clinton returned with most of the fleet to New York leaving Cornwallis to complete the mission in South Carolina. The march to North Carolina and Virginia would soon commence and Washington would be caught in a vise. Their *Southern Strategy* was working.

There was only one thing standing in their way – Francis Marion, the 47-year-old "*runt of the litter*" who would soon be dubbed, "*The Swamp Fox.*"

Chapter 28 ~ Camden

As Charleston was being threatened, Washington summoned Baron DeKalb, Lafayette's mentor and translator from his early days in America. Dekalb had been in charge of a regiment of Continentals and had been dispatched by Washington several times in and around New York and New Jersey but his men had not fired a shot. The Prussian Baron was now in his mid-fifties, and it was beginning to look like the American Revolution would pass him by. He had not seen Lafayette in more than a year.

Washington assigned DeKalb 1,400 men from Maryland and Delaware with a mission to assist in the defense of Charleston. These men had fought so well at Brooklyn that Washington thought they could make a difference in South Carolina. What's more, DeKalb had previously done a detailed inspection of Charleston's defenses in 1777 when he arrived with Lafayette. This would be DeKalb's chance.

Washington wrote to DeKalb on April 4 from Morristown. In his typically formal style, he gave him no instructions other than to hasten to Charleston.

"I wish you safe and expeditious march there and every success that you could possibly desire."

Washington had previously sent General Benjamin Lincoln's 6,000 largely untested troops from North Carolina to try and retake Savannah but that attempt had failed. Those men were now defending Charleston, and it was unclear to Washington what the situation was there. If DeKalb was to participate in the defense of Charleston, he needed to arrive quickly.

DeKalb left Philadelphia in late April.

In June 1780, he arrived at Cox's Mill, South Carolina, and learned that Charleston had already fallen. Now unattached, he decided to seek out Marion to join his command.

DeKalb had never met Marion but word of his exploits was starting to filter through the ranks. When DeKalb rode into Marion's camp, the South Carolina Colonel was skeptical of this Prussian.

Samuel was overjoyed to see DeKalb. They had not seen each other in quite some time. They saluted and then warmly embraced.

Samuel spoke to Marion about DeKalb's military experience, and it was agreed he would join the unit. It was additional manpower that Marion sorely needed, and they soon agreed on a plan of harassment against the British. Gates was in an unusual position. He had formally been elevated to the Continental Army after routing the British at Fort Sullivan in 1776 but he had continued to take orders from Moultrie, the head of the South Carolina militia. All of Marion's men, with the exception of Huger and DeKalb, were militia. In his mind, his loyalty was to the State of South Carolina.

Meanwhile, Washington had learned of the defeat in Charleston and sent General Horatio Gates, the hero of Monmouth Courthouse, with an additional 1,500 men. Gates connected with Marion and assumed command on August 1. Baron DeKalb, more respectful of the chain of command, deferred to Gates, but Marion had no use for this *"northern, empty uniform."* The feeling was mutual as Gates did not like Marion's appearance and lack of decorum. Samuel talked to Marion at length about Gates, having seen firsthand the Continental General's battlefield performances in places like Monmouth and Brandywine, but Francis Marion remained unimpressed.

"He does not know us, our people, our culture or, more importantly, the South Carolina fighting spirit. Most importantly, he does not know the terrain, our many creeks, rivers, swamps and marshland. South Carolina will teach him a hard lesson."

Gates, sensing Marion's disloyalty, sent him away into the interior of the state on a mission to destroy Cornwallis' river craft. Marion eagerly accepted and spent the month of July doing just that. Samuel Huger and Laurens' former soldiers were now part of Marion's 2nd Regiment and went with him. Baron DeKalb remained with Gates.

Two weeks later, on August 16, 1780, Gates decided to engage the British at Camden, South Carolina. It was another disaster for the Americans. The hated British Colonel, Banastre Tarleton swept around to the left of Gates' flank and attacked his men from behind. Gates' inexperienced troops from Virginia broke ranks and ran, with Gates himself fleeing from his tent in his nightclothes. In little more than an hour, 900 men under Gates' command were either killed or captured. Gates fled all the way to North Carolina and, with Marion gone, DeKalb assumed command.

[Crawford, 65]

DeKalb led a counter assault and found himself surrounded. In the end, he was dragged from his mount and bayoneted several times. Cornwallis, nearby, was summoned to help identify this unknown American commander.

Looking over DeKalb's field stretcher, Cornwallis remarked, "I am sorry, sir, to see you, not sorry that you are vanquished, but sorry to see you so badly wounded."

Clinton directed his own surgeons to see to DeKalb's wounds.

As he lay dying, DeKalb was reported to have said to a British officer, "I thank you, sir, for your generous sympathy but I die the death I always prayed for, the death of a soldier fighting for the rights of man."

He died three days later. He was 60 years old and died far from home on American soil. It would be several months before Lafayette would learn of his mentor's death.

With no effective leadership, another counter assault by the leaderless Americans at a place called Fishing Creek in October also resulted in a massive defeat.

The routs at Camden and Fishing Creek were another in a long line of humiliating American defeats. One thousand more American soldiers were killed or captured. There was nothing, now, to stop Cornwallis on his March north.

The *Southern Strategy* was in high gear.

Chapter 29 ~ Nelson's Ferry

Only by chance had Francis Marion avoided the disaster at Camden, on a "*fools' errand*" from Gates. But this was now his moment. With Gates gone, Marion was on his own. There was no organized opposition to Cornwallis in South Carolina.

Marion's broken ankle from that incident in Charleston in June was still causing him pain but he did not let that slow him down. He had no commanding officer and no orders. He wrote to Gates repeatedly but heard nothing. He had about 350 men including Samuel Huger's. His plan was simply to make life miserable for Cornwallis.

He sat down with his officers one night in their camp. These men he depended on now were from a variety of backgrounds. He looked them all squarely in the eye.

"I don't have to tell you we are in a difficult position. With Charleston in British hands, my commanding officer General Moultrie is a prisoner. Gates was sent here by Washington to assist but now he, too, is gone. I only knew Baron DeKalb briefly but he has died on South Carolina soil. We take orders from nobody. We decide who and when we attack. We will use the rivers and creeks of South Carolina to our advantage. We cannot defeat Cornwallis in an open assault, so we will bleed him a little at a time. We strike at night, in the dark and move on. We will make our British adversaries sorry they ever set foot in our state. Washington will eventually reinforce us."

Marion was badly outnumbered but he had some advantages. All of his men were mounted, giving him the upper hand in moving quickly from place to place. But his biggest advantage was geography. South Carolina is crisscrossed by several major rivers, the Pee Dee, the Santee, the Congaree and the Black, and countless wide creeks. Marion and his men knew them all ... the bends in the river, the shallows where you could cross on horseback, the remote islands offering shelter from the summer heat. His tactics would be to hit and run, attack at night, use the water as an asset, not a liability. If he could delay the British advance north, perhaps Washington would send reinforcements.

In August, Marion learned through an informer that 150 prisoners from the defeat at Camden under Gates were being held at Thomas Sumter's plantation house, a few miles from Nelson's Ferry on the Santee River. Sumter himself was a former Continental officer who had resigned his command. When Governor Rutledge fled Charleston, he appointed Sumter in charge of the South Carolina militia, but Sumter and his men seemed interested in only one thing – plunder. They were taking every opportunity to enrich themselves by stealing from South Carolina citizens. Sumter was in the upstate after being appointed by Rutledge, and Marion had not heard from him.

Cornwallis' men had dubbed Sumter, "*The Gamecock.*"

Cornwallis, fearing a smallpox epidemic among the prisoners captured in Charleston, had separated them into smaller groups before marching them on to prison ships in Charleston and Georgetown. These men at the Sumter plantation were lightly guarded by only 60 British troops. This would be a good place to start. Free the men and add them to his command.

But Marion only had about 150 troops with him at the moment, as much of his brigade under Peter Horry was still off burning Cornwallis' river rafts, and several dozen had gone home to tend to their farms. These were militia, part-time soldiers, not Continental soldiers. Most of Marion's force now consisted of Samuel Huger's company.

Should Marion wait for Horry to return or surprise the 60 guards at Sumter's plantation? He met with Samuel Huger.

"Lieutenant, we go tonight. Get your men ready."

Marion decided to attack at night, a tactic he would use over and over. But a British sentry discovered them approaching and fired a warning shot outside the plantation home. Marion then had only one option, attack. Samuel Huger led the charge with his company. He was pleasantly surprised to find the British sleeping inside the plantation home with their weapons neatly stacked outside. The fight was over in minutes. With the enemy fleeing into the swamp, Samuel's men captured 20 and two British were killed. All 150 Continentals, men from Maryland and Delaware, were freed.

[Oller, 54-55]

To Marion's surprise, only a handful of these men decided to join his force. Eighty-five left to join their original Continental regiment now somewhere in North Carolina. Sixty more disappeared into the South Carolina woods. But the raid was successful.

After the raid, he and his men moved to Witherspoon's Ferry, a spot called Britain's Neck. It was a strip of land between two rivers that he used as his base camp for the next few months. Camping on islands in the middle of rivers was another tactic Marion would effectively use.

He sent his Nelson's Ferry prisoners off to a Continental camp in Wilmington, North Carolina.

The Nelson's Ferry raid had a couple of other effects of note. Francis Marion suddenly came to the attention of Washington and the pro-American newspaper, the *Jersey Journal* in Chatham New Jersey. Hungry for good news from the south, they printed a short article in October (misspelling his name).

"Good news from South Carolina – The commander of the South Carolina 2nd Regiment, Francis Merion, conducted a successful raid on a British camp holding 150 Continental soldiers. All were freed unharmed and will be rejoining their regiments. Well done, Colonel Merion."

But Marion had now also come to the attention of Cornwallis. Before returning to New York, Clinton instructed Cornwallis to secure all of South Carolina and then go move on into North Carolina. In fact, three weeks before the Nelson's Ferry raid, Cornwallis had sent a note off to Clinton that South Carolina was secured. Now, he was not so sure. If men like Marion's could act against his forces with impunity, he had to wonder about the state of his control. His major supply lines across the many South Carolina rivers and creeks were now threatened. His boats had been burned and his prisoners freed. Maybe things were not as secure as he thought they were. He had to take action.

He issued the following order to all his officers,

"I have ordered in the most positive manner that every militia man who had borne arms with us and afterwards joined the enemy be immediately hanged."

He took one additional step rarely seen in military warfare. He specifically targeted an enemy commander, *"this Marion fellow,"* assigning his most vicious officer, Banastre Tarleton, to track down and kill Marion.

One day in September, after pursuing Marion for 26 miles through a dense South Carolina swamp, Tarleton proclaimed *"… as for this old fox, the Devil himself could not catch him."*

After that, everyone started to refer to Francis Marion as *"The Swamp Fox."* He smiled a bit when one of his men told him what Cornwallis had named him. His legend continued to grow as his exploits continued.

It was a good start but much more remained to be done.

Chapter 30 ~ Prisoner John Laurens

John Laurens was one of the 5,600 men captured at Charleston. He tried to hide his identity, but he was soon discovered to be a senior officer. Another prisoner, turned informant, told the British he was the son of Henry Laurens. With his hands bound behind him, John was taken to Cornwallis' headquarters in downtown Charleston. After Clinton's departure in July, Cornwallis had taken over Drayton Hall, one of the most palatial Charleston homes, as his headquarters.

Laurens was ushered into Cornwallis' office and the General directed that the prisoner's hands be untied. The guard then stood in the corner of the large office.

There was a certain protocol in place between the two armies during these times. Officers who were captured were to be treated with respect, asked if they would defect and be exchanged in a few months.

"Sit down, Colonel," Cornwallis directed, pointing to a chair at the side of his desk. He did not even look up from the document he was reading.

"Bring him some water and some fruit," Cornwallis directed to an orderly.

The two men then stared at each other. Each had read many reports about the other but they had never met. Cornwallis began, "Well, well, well, if it isn't the son of Henry Laurens. I am sorry to say you have chosen badly in this conflict which is about to end.

We have sent word to your father that you are unharmed but detained."

John Laurens looked at this man steely-eyed.

"You may have prevailed at the moment, sir, but rest assured this conflict is far from over. You have overreached by thrusting your forces into my home state and you will soon pay dearly. Enjoy your momentary respite in the home of one of my friends and prepare for what comes next."

Cornwallis sat back and smiled as he contemplated this brash young man. John Laurens was mostly bluster right now and Cornwallis knew it. The young American colonel had no idea what the overall American military situation was now, but he did know that the British did not understand South Carolina.

The fruit and water were brought in and placed on a small table beside Laurens. He ignored it, staring straight at Cornwallis.

"You and the other officers will be moved to one of your father's plantations along the river that we have captured. We will provide you the means to write to your father in Philadelphia. I expect he will demand your immediate release, and we will see about that. Now, I must leave for what you call 'the upstate' where we plan to eliminate what is left of Washington's forces. Good day, sir."

With that, John Laurens, prisoner of war, was ushered out and taken by wagon to one his father's eight plantations, an irony devised by Cornwallis' second in command, Banastre Tarleton.

He wrote to his wife Matilde, in London, careful with his words, knowing his captors would read it before sending it on.

"My dearest – I am saddened to tell you that I am currently detained by the British in Charleston, South Carolina. I am well cared for by General Cornwallis and hope to be set free soon. Do not worry about me. I long for the day that we are together again. This time apart will only strengthen us.

Yours, John."

He would remain there for three months and then be released, promising in writing not to take up arms against the British ever again. He was released in December 1780 in Philadelphia with the agreement he would also not leave Pennsylvania.

Chapter 31 ~ Rochambeau

While Marion was just starting to wreak havoc in the south, the French fleet with Admiral Rochambeau in charge left France for America. On July 11, 1780, they were spotted outside of Newport, Rhode Island, and messages were quickly sent to Washington in Philadelphia. This was desperately needed good news coming on the heels of the fall of Charleston and Gates' subsequent routs at Camden and Fishing Creek.

Washington dispatched Lafayette to open the discussions with Rochambeau and made plans for them to meet. The young aide and Washington met in Philadelphia in July.

"Colonel Lafayette, you have served me well and I wish you to open the discussions with General Rochambeau. I don't know him but I believe you do from your years in France. Clinton has not yet returned with the fleet from Charleston, and we have a narrow opportunity to attack a weakened New York."

Washington had longed to take back New York since his ignominious defeat at Brooklyn four years earlier.

"But we must meet soon to coordinate a plan. I am counting on you. Gain his agreement on the New York plan and arrange for us to meet."

"Yes, sir, I know Rochambeau well from my recent time in France. He is an honorable man and a capable commander. I will inform him of your wishes and establish a time and place for you to meet."

Lafayette left that day and a week later, met with the French aboard the flagship off Newport. The meeting did not go well. Rochambeau informed him that he had with him only 4,000 men, not the 6,000 that Lafayette had been told would make the trip. In addition, most of the men were sick and malnourished from the arduous crossing and would not be fit to fight for at least two months. What was worse was that the additional ships carrying the desperately needed arms, supplies, uniforms and munitions for the Continental Army were still back in France, delayed by supply line issues. Rochambeau held out no promise of the quick action that Washington desired.

Lafayette drafted a summary of the meeting trying to put a positive spin on the discussion, inaccurately referring to his own role and influence in the decision. To Rochambeau, the young Lafayette was an errand boy, not a seasoned diplomat. Questioning the judgment of the French commander, Lafayette's personal interest in action got the better of him. He wrote, "*From an intimate knowledge of our situation ... it is important for us to act during the current campaign ... to avoid the fatal consequences of inaction.*"

Rochambeau, highly insulted, replied simply that he would be happy to meet with the American Commander to privately relay his own thoughts.

Lafayette quickly wrote a letter of apology and Rochambeau, an old family friend of Lafayette's in-laws, accepted the apology. A meeting was arranged in Hartford with Washington.

[Duncan, 110-113]

Throughout the summer of 1780, details of the losses in Charleston streamed in and the numbers were staggering. Nearly 6,000 Continentals taken prisoner, among them John Laurens and Benjamin Lincoln. Washington eagerly arranged to meet with the French commander in September.

The Hartford meetings were cordial but not of much conse-quence, with Lafayette acting as translator. Clinton was, by then, back in New York, so attacking him there was no longer an option. But Rochambeau and his senior staff were awe-struck by Washing-ton. His presence and demeanor lived up to his reputation.

The Americans were told a British naval blockade in the English Channel would impede the arrival of more ships with supplies for several months. Winter was approaching and they agreed to re-sume discussions in early 1781. The year would end with the status quo in the North.

On the way back from Hartford, Washington's entourage stopped at West Point where Benedict Arnold, the hero of Ticonderoga in 1777, had recently been appointed as commander. The fort sat on an elevated bluff controlling the Hudson River below, a vital as-set of the Americans. But while preparing for dinner one night, Arnold was absent. Suddenly, word was brought to Lafayette that a British officer in civilian clothes had been apprehended by some local militia nearby. His name was Major John Andre and, upon interrogating him, it was discovered that he had detailed plans of West Point in his boots and that they had been provided to him by Arnold. Benedict Arnold was a traitor who had sold out West Point for a promised commission in the British Army! By the time Lafayette got back to inform Washington, Arnold was aboard a British boat fleeing down the Hudson to New York City, leaving his wife behind to explain his absence.

Lafayette and Arnold would encounter each other in the not-too-distant future in the American south.

Chapter 32 ~ Tory Opposition

After Nelson's Ferry, Marion was a marked man. Banastre Tarleton was assigned by Cornwallis to kill him and another British officer Major William Wemyss, a Scotsman, also received orders from Cornwallis to "*disarm in the most rigid manner*" sympathizers with Marion's supporters. Cornwallis needed to settle this South Carolina situation quickly and move north into North Carolina to achieve the *Southern Strategy*.

In late August, Marion received word that a force of 250 Loyalist militia, under the command of a man named Ganey, were marching in his direction. Marion had only 90 men under his command at that time as many had returned home to tend to their farms and families. But Samuel Huger and his company were still with Marion.

Ganey was a former Continental officer who switched sides over an affront from an American superior. His militia wore no standard uniforms and, like Marion's men, were all dressed differently. Marion directed his men to wear a white feather in their caps, so as to tell friend from foe in the midst of battle.

He encountered Ganey's men at a place called Blue Savannah, along the Pee Dee River, so named for the bluish swamp mud prevalent in the area.

Positioning Samuel Huger's sharpshooters on both sides of the road, Marion's militia attacked and feigned a retreat back down the road. Ganey's men pursued and Samuel's men caught them in an ambush, inflicting heavy casualties. Ganey's men fled all the way back to Georgetown. Marion's casualty toll—one man wounded and two horses dead!

When word of this latest Marion rout reached Cornwallis, he was infuriated and assigned two more death squads to track down and kill "*The Swamp Fox.*"

"This Marion fellow must be extinguished," he screamed at his subordinates.

 Ninety new volunteers showed up, bringing Marion's strength to 180.

What began then was a sort of reign of terror on both sides. The British Commander William Wemyss began a program of torching rebel plantations and homes, telling Cornwallis in early September that he had "*burned 20 plantations and 50 rebel homes.*" Marion's men began their own series of home fires torching one Tory home after another.

In mid-September, Marion learned that three separate forces were converging on his position. His instinct was to stand and fight but he realized how badly he was outnumbered and withdrew at the last minute all the way north across the North Carolina border.

Cornwallis concluded, incorrectly, that South Carolina was now finally secure.

But Marion was far from done. In late September, he learned of another Tory camp at a place called Black Mingo Creek on the Pee Dee River. Its water is colored by tannin, giving it the color of tea. It was led by a militia commander named John Corning Ball, who was related by marriage to Marion.

Marion studied the terrain and realized he would have to travel some distance south from North Carolina, over several creeks and rivers to reach the enemy camp.

He met with his two senior officers, Samuel Huger and Colonel Peter Horry.

"I've decided this will be a night raid. We must be very careful. The bridges we cross must be covered in blankets before we cross lest our horses alert our foes. Get your men rested, we leave at sunset."

It was a moonless night and Marion's mounted men crossed one bridge after another, spreading soft blankets ahead of them to muffle the sound of the horses. All South Carolinians knew how sound carries at night across creeks and swamps. At one point, Marion's men waded across a creek that had no bridge. They found the enemy camp with some difficulty, attacking from two directions. The Loyalist militia, once again, fled into the swamp. Many of the British sympathizers were killed and, more importantly, Marion's men captured vast supplies and ammunition. Marion himself captured Ball's fine horse, renaming it "Ball" and rode it for the rest of the war.

For a time, this raid had the effect of stopping all further Tory opposition in South Carolina.

Cornwallis, in an effort to shield his own men from blame, reported to Clinton, "*I have found our militia here to fail so totally when put to the trial in this province (SC).*"

[Oller, 69-71]

Chapter 33 ~ King's Mountain

After Cornwallis' resounding victory at Camden in the late summer of 1780, he became convinced that South Carolina had been subjugated. He began to make plans to move his operation to North Carolina. But he had to ensure that the upstate of South Carolina on his left flank was secure. He gave that assignment to Major Patrick "Bull Dog" Ferguson. The force he commanded was 1,100 almost entirely Loyalist militia who remained loyal to the king. But word of his presence spread among the border communities between North and South Carolina. An American militia commander name William Campbell had already organized a force of what were called "*Overmountain Men.*" Earlier that summer, this group had beaten back loyalists in small skirmishes at places like Thicketty Fort, Cedar Springs and Musgrove's Mill, all in South Carolina.

When Ferguson set up his camp on King's Mountain, he sent messengers into the local communities that they should "*desist from opposition to British arms.*"

Those messages did not have the intended effect and Campbell decided it was time for action. Men like John Sevier and Benjamin Cleveland, who had read about Francis Marion's tactics and success, rallied to Campbell's call and 900 *Overmountain Men* showed up, muskets in hand.

Compared to other battles during the War of Independence, this was small but it proved to be one of the most savage, pitting Americans against Americans.

On October 5, 1780, they met. In the hours preceding the clash, Campbell's men intercepted a 14-year-old boy who had an encoded message for Cornwallis. He quickly translated it, and the message provided Campbell with exact positions and even detailed the checkered shirt that Ferguson would be wearing over his uniform in battle.

Campbell's men had marched all night in the rain but were ready to attack in the morning, surrounding Ferguson's forces on all four sides. It is believed that Ferguson was the only non-American on the hill that morning.

The rebels put green sprigs on their hats so as to distinguish themselves from the British Tories and the fighting was intense. The four rebel companies all reached the summit simultaneously and Ferguson's forces dropped back. As he rode around trying to rally them, he was shot from his horse, propped up against a tree, and died. With their commanding officer gone, the rest of the Tory loyalists quickly surrendered.

At that moment, a force of 2,200 of Ferguson's men who had been out on a foraging mission returned and this was interpreted by the rebels as a counter attack. Vicious fighting recommenced and another hundred were killed. Outraged, rebels passed by Ferguson's lifeless body and stuck bayonets in him. Sevier took his silk sash and Cleveland took his horse.

The American rebels lost 90 men that day with 60 more wounded.

The British Tories had 157 killed, including Ferguson, who had been shot seven times, 163 wounded, and 700 captured.

When word of this disaster reached Cornwallis, he abandoned his plans to move his forces to Charlotte. Things were still unsettled in South Carolina. This Marion fellow was wreaking havoc in the Lowcountry and the Overmountain Men were in control in the upstate.

[Crawford, 119-130]

Chapter 34 ~ Snow's Island

Word of Marion's successes in the Lowcountry continued to spread in late 1780 and the British angst was peaking. King's Mountain was a major setback. Cornwallis was now under increased pressure from Clinton to advance the *Southern Strategy* but he was at a loss. The British general was already planning to move his headquarters to Charlotte following a spring offensive in North Carolina, but Marion had other plans back in South Carolina and the upstate was clearly unsettled with these Overmountain Men.

Wemyss and Tarleton were now spending most of their time trying to kill or capture Marion with no success.

The Swamp Fox made his winter camp on Snow's Island, South Carolina, near Florence. The Snow's Island camp was his pride and joy. It was a triangular shaped plateau in the middle of the Pee Dee River at the confluence of Lynches Creek. The camp was built for Marion by a local surveyor and landowner, and it was impenetrable. Marion's men then built earthworks or "redoubts" further strengthening the position. It was high and dry, protected on three sides by water and on the fourth by a deep pine forest. With game in the forest and fish in the river, Marion's men ate well that winter.

[Crawford, 224]

But a malaria outbreak in the camp in December took the life of Peter Horry, Marion's second-in-command, making Samuel Huger Marion's senior reporting officer. But Samuel now had other ideas.

Since the loss of John Laurens the previous summer, Samuel had accomplished much under Marion but his men were longing to return to rejoin the Continentals in the north. He then learned the Marquis de Lafayette had recently arrived in Virginia. Samuel immediately told Marion he planned to rejoin his old friend in the spring.

At the end of September, Marion was promoted by Governor Rutledge of South Carolina to Brigadier General in the South Carolina militia, symbolic perhaps, but it further enhanced Marion's reputation.

By December, Marion had given up on hearing anything from his former commander, Horatio Gates. He had written several notes to the Continental general asking for instructions. What Marion did not yet know was that Gates already had been replaced. Washington had selected Brigadier General Nathanael Greene. But it would be some time before Greene would arrive in South Carolina. In the meantime, Marion was still on his own.

Greene was a reluctant appointee. When he received word from Washington about the assignment, he wrote to his wife back in Rhode Island, "*What I have been dreading has come to pass.*"

Nathanael Greene had been with Washington from the beginning – New York, Washington Heights, and the retreat across New Jersey. He crossed the Delaware on that frozen night and led Washington's left flank against the Hessians in Trenton, capturing 1,200. He took over the following summer at Monmouth Courthouse and was at Brandywine. He was eventually appointed Quartermaster of the Continental Army, probably the most frustrating of all of Washington's appointments.

Greene was raised as a Quaker in Rhode Island but rejected those severe religious constraints as a young man. Smallpox disfigured one eye and he walked with a limp. He did not come from wealth or military heritage but had grown to be Washington's most trusted general. Now, in late 1780, he was entrusted with the most critical assignment, stopping the British in South Carolina.

Before Greene left, he asked Washington if he could visit his wife in Rhode Island. Washington declined writing him, *"Your presence with your command in the Carolinas as soon as possible is indispensable."*

He then asked Washington if he had any advice for him. Uncharacteristically, Washington admitted he knew little of the environment into which he was sending his general.

"Uninformed as I am of the enemy's force in that quarter, I can give you no particular instructions but must leave you to govern yourself entirely to your own prudence and judgment."

[Crawford, 145-146]

1780 had been a bloody year in South Carolina. More than 700 South Carolina soldiers had died, and 90% of all Americans wounded in the War of Independence in that year were wounded in South Carolina. Thousands more had been captured.

But 1781 would be even worse.

[Oller, 108]

Chapter 35 ~ Henry Laurens Captured

In early August 1780, Henry Laurens boarded a fast packet ship, *The Mercury*, out of Philadelphia. He had resigned as President of the Continental Congress after serving for a one-year term. His plantation homes and businesses had been destroyed in South Carolina, and he wanted to see if he could resurrect them. But Congress had one more assignment for him. He was named Minister to Holland. His mission aboard *The Mercury* was to secure a treaty and a loan from the government of Holland so that America to continue to finance the war. Dutifully, he accepted the assignment.

The Mercury was escorted out of Philadelphia by a heavily armed but much slower war vessel, *The Saratoga*. They sailed without incident down the Delaware River, putting out to sea off the coast of New York City. When they reached Newfoundland, *The Saratoga*, not outfitted for trans-Atlantic voyage, dropped off, returning to Boston. *The Mercury* was on her own.

One week later, on September 3, 1780, *The Mercury* was overtaken by a British frigate, *The Vestal*. The American ship had been running before its pursuer for more than five hours but a volley of cannon fire convinced her captain that escape was not possible. As the British approached *The Mercury*, Laurens instructed his assistant to throw his trunk of papers overboard. One of the British sailors spotted it. Unfortunately, the trunk did not sink and was quickly retrieved.

Once the British boarded, they quickly learned that *The Mercury* was bound for Holland, and there was an American passenger of note – Henry Laurens, the former President of the Continental Congress. The contents of the floating trunk were of great interest. Among the papers was a draft of a proposed treaty between America and Holland. Laurens was now the foreign minister to Holland, and he was traveling to negotiate an agreement with the Dutch, who were supposedly neutral in these global conflicts, interested only in making a profit. Laurens was taken prisoner, escorted to Newfoundland and then England.

Once in London, Henry Laurens was tried, convicted of treason, and imprisoned in the Tower of London. The War of Independence was over for Henry Laurens. It would be some time before his son, imprisoned in South Carolina, learned any of this.

But while in prison, Henry befriended the daughter of his jailer who brought him his meals each day. Throughout his imprisonment, she smuggled his correspondence in and out, allowing him to stay in touch with his colleagues. In a few months, he learned that his son, John, was also a British prisoner.

Once aware of the plans that Holland was making to aid America, England declared war on Holland further widening the global conflict.

Chapter 36 ~ Philadelphia, 1781

As the winter of 1780-1781 set in, Washington's "three sons" were reunited back in Philadelphia. Lafayette was back from his year in France, determined more than ever to fight for America's freedom. Hamilton was still holding things together with Washington, negotiating with Congress. John Laurens, now on parole from his capture in Charleston, was bound by his agreement not to take up arms against the British.

None of them knew it but Samuel Huger was fighting valiantly with Francis Marion in South Carolina.

Under the terms of his parole, John Laurens had been forced to sign an agreement that he would remain in Philadelphia and not take up arms. He had reluctantly signed and then immediately made plans to get back into uniform.

The three Washington aides began their regular meetings again and at the end of each, regaled each other with tales of battle. They had all been wounded, recovered and seen the highs and lows of Washington's campaigns. The more recent stories infuriated Hamilton who, by now, was chafing at the inaction of his current assignment with Washington.

One day, a tall young man was introduced to them. His name was Nate Muchmore, a former Washington spy who was now a journalist with the popular newspaper, *The Jersey Journal*. The *Journal* was the only pro-American newspaper in the Colonies, published by a man named Shepherd Kollock in Chatham, New Jersey. Nate

Muchmore was assigned to interview these three Washington aides who were gaining notoriety across the Colonies.

Nate settled into the chair that Samuel used to sit in among all the papers in Hamilton's tiny office. Lafayette, Laurens, and Hamilton read the *Journal* each week and were pleased with the honest portrayal of the American cause. The paper, naturally, downplayed American losses while emphasizing the few American victories.

Nate asked each of the aides pointed questions about Washington and his generals. He sat back and allowed each man to talk. Hamilton took the lead in describing each general, embellishing their military acumen and accomplishments. Muchmore then directed questions at each of three aides personally, their families, backgrounds, lives in the camps and battlefield experiences. All three young men had been wounded and Nate asked about that. He asked about their wives and children, whom they rarely, if ever, saw. Laurens had never even met his daughter, back in London. Lafayette had spent the last year in Paris with his wife Adrienne and his young daughter, and he had another child on the way. His wife was distraught when her husband left, again, for the Colonies and Lafayette spoke honestly about that. Hamilton was recently married to Elizabeth Schuyler, the daughter of New York Governor, Phillip Schuyler.

Nate's style was easygoing, and he let each man talk at length. He took many notes and would later recall small things he had been unable to write down. One thing he noted was how each of these three men seemed comfortable with each other.

When it was done, he stood and saluted each man since Nate, as a lieutenant, was junior to all of them in the Continental Army. This would not be their last meeting.

The next week, the interview appeared in the *Jersey Journal*. It was nearly a full page, unusual for that publication. Some of what Nate wrote read:

"… These three young officers came together at a time when Washington needed them the most. They had complete access to the Commander in Chief and would advise him daily on matters of war, politics with Congress, morale in the camps and strategies of the enemy. They are an invaluable resource for General Washington …"

Chapter 37 ~ The Three Sons Depart

In January 1781, Congress decided that they needed another voice in Paris to assist Franklin. When Lafayette was there, he tried and had made some progress using his family connections to the Court. But nothing formal had been decided by the king.

The supplies and, more importantly, funds that the Americans so desperately needed to keep the war going were hung up in French bureaucracy, and it was unclear if they would ever arrive. The attempt to borrow from the Dutch ended up with Henry Laurens in the Tower of London. The logical choice was to send Hamilton but Congress was much more familiar with John Laurens, the son of their former President. His argument about emancipation had impressed many members of Congress. He struck them as an effective diplomat, despite his age.

John Laurens was selected and neither he nor Hamilton was happy about it. Laurens boarded a ship bound for France out of Boston in late December and was in Paris by late January. His good-bye to his comrades, Hamilton and Lafayette, was abrupt and unemotional. It was not clear if they would ever see each other again.

Not long after that, Hamilton had concluded that his time with Washington had run its course. He wanted a military command. Washington repeatedly denied him saying that he was invaluable as an aide so Hamilton was looking for an excuse to leave. In February, interpreting an off-hand Washington comment as an affront, he resigned, leaving the Commander-in-Chief's side for the first time in four years, and moved to a small cabin on the Hudson with his wife Elizabeth to write his memoirs.

Lafayette was also ready to leave. He asked for and received a light infantry command and was sent to Virginia. Benedict Arnold, now a British General, was wreaking havoc with Virginians, burning and pillaging the countryside. Washington, still seething over Armold's treason, sent Lafayette after the traitor with unusually specific orders to track him down and hang him.

"Colonel, I ask that you take a command to Virginia and apprehend and detain Mr. Arnold, who has recently deceived our Country and brought shame."

Lafayette left in early March and was in Virginia in two weeks.

So, by March 1781, Samuel Huger and the three Washington aides were scattered once again. Huger was in South Carolina with Marion, Laurens in Paris, Lafayette in Virginia, and Hamilton in isolation on the Hudson. They were all destined to be together later that year.

Chapter 38 ~ Huger Departs

Francis Marion was a wanted man. His string of victories in the fall of 1780 had stopped Cornwallis dead in his tracks in South Carolina, just when it looked like nothing could stop the British march to North Carolina and Virginia. Cornwallis had assigned no fewer than six companies of men to track down and kill Marion. None was successful.

The two most prominent were General William Wemyss and Lieutenant-Colonel Banastre Tarleton, both of whom had reputations for torching homes and cruelty to American citizens.

After the rout at Camden, Marion sent several messages to his commanding officer, General Gates, but The Swamp Fox had no way of knowing Gates had run back all the way to Philadelphia where he was relieved of his command.

With no commanding officer, Francis Marion had been free to act on his own. He would continue to select his own British targets and tactics, a strategy that played to his strengths.

With word of his success, Marion's ranks had now swelled to several hundred as volunteers kept showing up at his camp, wanting to get in on the action. Samuel Huger had kept his unit together under Marion all these months but when he learned that Lafayette was now in Virginia, he felt bound to reconnect his men to a formal Continental Army regiment. His assignment to Marion was of his own choosing after escaping Charleston, so he met with Marion one evening in March in their hidden camp in the swamps.

"Colonel, my time here has run its course. I am grateful to you for taking me and my men in after Charleston, but it is time I rejoined the Continentals in the north. I request your permission to join Lafayette in Virginia."

Marion had never met Lafayette but knew of him by reputation. Losing Huger would have an impact, but he was ready to promote two of his nephews and the new volunteers had filled in Marion's ranks.

They sat on logs across from each other with a campfire between them. They were both South Carolina natives but from vastly different backgrounds. Samuel was from an aristocratic rice plantation family, and Marion was from a basic working man's family. They had, however, a common French Huguenot heritage.

Marion could see that Samuel's mind was made up. Even if Marion denied him, as a Continental officer, Samuel was within his rights to leave and rejoin his old regiment.

"Bonne chance, Lieutenant," as Marion lapsed back into their common boyhood language. They stood, saluted and shook hands.

"I am sorry about your father. I knew Benjamin Huger to be a fine man and outstanding militia officer."

"Thank you, sir."

Samuel met with his company that night. He told them to prepare to leave and that they would continue the fight closer to home. Welcome news.

Chapter 39 ~ Benedict Arnold

Shortly after defecting from West Point to the British, Benedict Arnold was assigned 2,000 British Redcoats and sent to Portsmouth, Virginia. Anxious to please his new British masters, he marched into Richmond unopposed and set fire to much of the city. He was soon joined by 2,000 more soldiers from New York led by General William Phillips. Lafayette did not know it at the time, but Phillips was the man who had killed his father years earlier in the Seven Years War. Long after the war, he would discover that.

Washington sent Lafayette to Virginia with only 900 men, all that he could spare. His mission was to kill or capture Arnold.

Soon after that, Samuel Huger arrived from South Carolina with his small company. He and Lafayette warmly greeted each other. They had not seen each other since Laurens and Samuel left Philadelphia for South Carolina in the spring of 1780.

"What word of Colonel Laurens?" Samuel asked Lafayette.

"We were all afraid he had been killed at Charleston but he was apparently captured. As an officer, he was paroled but, with his father's role in Congress and imprisonment, it was complicated. John is now in Paris with Franklin negotiating on our behalf."

They then spoke at length about South Carolina and the impact Francis Marion was having.

Samuel told him, "He is like no military leader you have known before. His stature belies his leadership, and his tactics infuriate the British. I don't know where we would be without him."

Word was then received that Thomas Jefferson, Governor of Virginia, was sending 1,500 local militia to augment Lafayette's forces. Jefferson had promised 3,000 but held back, thinking that his first priority was to defend his own interests. In addition, General Anthony Wayne was on his way with another 1,000 men. Lafayette would soon be on even footing with Benedict Arnold.

Lafayette tracked Arnold across Virginia but was unable to engage him. It was a game of cat and mouse, and Lafayette was waiting for the right opportunity to pounce. That opportunity would never come.

Cornwallis, frustrated at his lack of success in South Carolina, now believed Virginia held the key, with the deep-water Chesapeake Bay in which his Navy could maneuver.

In late April 1781, Cornwallis abandoned Charleston, forgot about North Carolina and headed to Virginia, leaving small garrisons behind at Charleston and Savannah. Once in Virginia, he assumed command of Benedict Arnold's troops, bringing his force to 7,000 Redcoats. Benedict Arnold returned to New York and never fought against Americans again. For Cornwallis, everything now was focusing on Virginia.

In June, Lord Germain, back in London, wrote,

"I am well pleased to find that Lord Cornwallis' opinion coincides entirely with mine of the great importance of pushing the war on the side of Virginia, with all the forces that can be spared, until that province is reduced."

[Greene, 7-8]

Cornwallis was expecting Clinton would supply him with additional forces from New York but that never happened.

Cornwallis had to deal with Lafayette and his 2,000 men in Richmond, the new state capital, so he marched 5,300 of his men there. Cornwallis wrote to Clinton, *"I will catch the boy."*

It was not clear now who was the hunter and who was the hunted. Cornwallis was hunting Lafayette, and Lafayette was hunting Arnold. With Cornwallis reinforced, Lafayette was outnumbered and somewhat apprehensive of Cornwallis' reputation as a clever strategist and field commander. In late June, Lafayette learned that Benedict Arnold had left Virginia and returned to New York, so he began to focus on Cornwallis.

Cornwallis had left the south in ruins. Cities bombarded, plantations plundered, bridges destroyed, fields barren not having been planted in the spring. It was starting to look like both South Carolina and Georgia might not recover. South Carolina, in particular, had little left of its once bustling economy. Charleston was almost completely shut down with the British occupation. Now, he was planning to do the same to Virginia.

[Crawford, This Fierce People, 271-273]

Lafayette then made a strategic decision. He had listened over and over to Samuel Huger's descriptions of Marion's tactics, engaging superior forces with a smaller army. Lafayette decided that, until Washington could reinforce him with assistance from the French, he would *"skirmish and not engage too far."*

Washington augmented Lafayette's forces first with troops under General Anthony Wayne and then with more under Baron Von Steuben. Lafayette was now a major general with 4,000 men under his command.

It was then that Cornwallis hatched a plan to capture Governor Thomas Jefferson. He dispatched the hated Banastre Tarleton who brought several hundred Redcoats with him to Charlottesville, close to Jefferson's residence at Monticello. But Lafayette, who was now following Cornwallis' movements, learned of the plan and dispatched Samuel to warn Jefferson.

Samuel arrived at Monticello and was escorted by Virginia militia guards into the estate house.

Jefferson was at his desk, deeply engaged in some papers in front of him.

"Sir, forgive the intrusion. My name is Samuel Huger, lieutenant under the command of General Lafayette."

Jefferson looked up, somewhat annoyed.

"Yes, Lieutenant, what can I do for you?"

"I am here to inform you of the imminent presence of British dragoons in Charlottesville on a mission to capture you. You must evacuate immediately."

Thomas Jefferson looked up, calmly walked to his porch, took out a telescope and trained it down the hill to Charlottesville in the distance. There he observed British soldiers laying waste to the town. To Samuel's amazement, the Governor calmly walked back to his desk and began sorting through various papers saving the most critical in a wooden crate. There seemed to be no urgency on his part.

They evacuated within the hour and when the British arrived, Monticello was unoccupied. Tarleton, who was infamous for torching every American building he encountered, ordered his men to leave the Monticello estate and its furnishings as they found it.

Years later Jefferson wrote simply in his memoirs,

"British horse came to Monticello June 4, 1781."

Cornwallis then located and destroyed another Jefferson residence at Elk Hill. He did not exercise the same constraint as Tarleton had at Monticello and burned it to the ground before retreating east, eventually to Yorktown. Cornwallis took 30 of Jefferson's slaves with him and would later use them against the Americans.

As Lafayette engaged and retreated, Cornwallis received orders from New York. Clinton became aware of the French Navy's planned move to the Chesapeake, so he ordered Cornwallis to move upriver and establish a winter base at Yorktown.

Cornwallis resisted and continued to play cat-and-mouse with Lafayette. Lafayette wrote to Washington that his strategy with Cornwallis was that of "*a terrier baiting a bull*."

They did eventually engage near Jamestown, Virginia, in early July 1781. In what was called "The Battle of the Green Spring," Lafayette dispatched "Mad Anthony" Wayne to attack what he thought was Cornwallis' rear guard. But the shrewd British general outmaneuvered Wayne at the cost of 140 American lives.

But Lafayette was not about to back off. He kept at Cornwallis, forcing him up the peninsula. It was now late July and Cornwallis dispatched his Royal Engineers to re-assess Yorktown. The village sat high on a bluff overlooking the York River with Gloucester Point on the opposite bank, one mile away. Cornwallis was surprised at the engineers' report.

Yorktown was a deep-water station, deep enough to accommodate the heaviest British warships. Moreover, Gloucester Point narrowed the channel, pointing down river and affording excellent gun positions for any naval assault. Finally, the land side of Yorktown was cut with deep ravines, providing solid defense against any land attack.

Cornwallis was sold. By late August, he was moving the Southern British Army of 7,000 into Yorktown. Clinton could resupply and reinforce him in the spring of 1782 and complete the *Southern Strategy*.

It was a move that would prove crucial in the American War of Independence.

[Greene, 10-14]

Chapter 40 ~ *The Bridges Campaign, 1781*

With Samuel gone, Marion needed to promote some junior officers to fill the void, and he did that with two of his nephews. In the meantime, a new Marion adversary had emerged, assigned to kill or capture him. His name was John Watson Tadwell-Watson.

He was a difficult man to deal with, a lieutenant-colonel in the British 3rd Regiment. As Cornwallis was planning to leave South Carolina, he assigned Watson to track down and kill Marion and subdue all the South Carolina militia between Camden and Georgetown. Watson started by building a fort on a high bluff on the Santee River and named it Fort Watson.

On March 7, 1781, Watson marched out of that fort with 500 Redcoats, veterans of the fighting in New York and New Jersey. He also had with him a regiment of South Carolina Tory militia, many of whom had, at one time, been fighting on the other side for the Americans.

Marion quickly learned of the approaching British force. He had with him only 400 men, all mounted South Carolinians. In mid-morning, at a place called Wyboo Swamp (near present-day Manning), Marion and Watson faced each other, sitting atop their horses, on either side of a wide creek with an earthen causeway dike. They stared across at each other knowing what was coming.

This would be Marion's ultimate test. No hit and run, no surprise nighttime assaults, no ambush, no retreat. Marion's men, for the first time, would be tested in open battle.

Marion could not, however, resist the temptation to use deception. Positioning his cavalry hidden in a swamp, Marion attacked and then retreated, drawing the British in. Marion's men struck and chased the British back but encountered something that Marion had not seen before. British cannon fire. Watson only had two field pieces with him but they sprayed Marion's men with metal fragments, turning the tide of battle to the British. Men and horses fell in this barrage. A bayonet charge by the British was then repelled by the Americans, and the battle continued back and forth all day. In fact, the engagement would last two more weeks and would come to be known as the Marion Bridges Campaign.

The contest went back and forth over bridges and swamps along the Black and Santee rivers between Kingstree and Georgetown. During the engagements, Marion and Watson exchanged several letters, each complaining about the others' tactics.

At one point, the two military leaders arranged a prisoner exchange. The exchange was to take place in Georgetown but, when the American lead negotiator arrived under a white flag, he was taken prisoner by Watson's men. And so, it went on.

A few days later, as the cat-and-mouse game continued, Watson's men were planning to cross the Black River at Lower Bridge. Dismantling the planks in the bridge, Marion's men positioned themselves on the far bank. Marion's men were backwoods farmers and were very accurate with their long rifles. With the bridge out, the British tried to cross at a shallow ford but Marion's sharpshooters inflicted heavy casualties. Watson retreated and the letter writing commenced once again. By March 20, Watson tried to cross at the Sampit River bridge, nine miles from Georgetown. Once again, Marion's men disabled the bridge. Watson, again, ordered his men to wade across. Twenty more died at the hands of Marion's sharpshooters and Watson himself had his horse shot from under him. Watson would finally, reluctantly, withdraw, his men exhausted from the three-week fight. He pulled his forces back to Fort Watson.

He wrote to Cornwallis, "*These South Carolinians will not sleep and fight like gentlemen.*"

[Oller, 137-140]

The Bridges Campaign ended by March 22, 1781, with Marion's reputation further enhanced. But his men were exhausted only to find out that their safe-haven camp at Snow's Island had been discovered and destroyed. Marion held a council with his senior officers and all his men in attendance on horseback surrounding them. It was a leadership style not seen before in military circles. He would let his men decide what their next step would be.

He spoke to them turning often to face each mounted group.

Should they disburse to defend their homesteads or remain with the Swamp Fox as he retreated to yet another new camp in North Carolina? Marion made an impassioned plea for patriotism, one of the few times that he made a speech. When he was done, he sat down on a log and there was a long moment of silence.

His officers and men unanimously agreed that they would follow him north. Soon, more encouraging news arrived.

General Gates' replacement, General Nathanael Greene, had marched south from Philadelphia and stopped Cornwallis at Guilford Courthouse in North Carolina. Greene would soon be coming back to South Carolina to help Marion liberate the state.

Chapter 41 ~ The War of Posts

Frances Marion and his militia were now part of Greene's Continental Army but they had yet to meet. They corresponded frequently with Greene requesting assistance and intelligence about Cornwallis' whereabouts.

Greene started by asking Marion to send him 50 negroes with corn and rice for his soldiers in North Carolina. Marion complied but managed to do it in a way that was minimally disruptive to his fellow South Carolinians.

For weeks, notes went back and forth by courier between Greene and Marion.

Marion then informed Greene of something he had just learned. A British force of 1,500 soldiers had arrived in Charleston that past December from New York under the command of General Alexander Leslie. Leslie immediately departed for the interior upstate of South Carolina with orders to connect with Cornwallis in North Carolina. Marion kept Greene apprised of all this.

[Oller, 110]

Greene soon realized what Marion had always known. To be an effective force in the Carolinas required horses, and all of Marion's men were mounted. Most of Greene's men were on foot. Crossing the many creeks and streams in the south would be a constant challenge.

Greene wrote to his colleagues in the north, "*... this country is* *full of deep rivers and impassable creeks and swamps, that you are always liable to misfortunes of a capital nature."*

Greene was a student of topography and was constantly studying maps, such as they were in 1781. In eastern South Carolina, bridges were few and rivers difficult to ford, with most men unable to swim. But horses could swim.

Greene requested Marion send him more horses on multiple occasions but Marion, with none to spare, ignored the additional requests. Marion's cavalry leader agreed with Marion and the issue nearly ruptured the relationship between Greene and Marion.

[Oller, 113]

In an attempt to smooth things over, Greene sent Marion much needed ammunition and, to Marion's enormous gratitude, 250 Continental soldiers under Lieutenant Colonel Henry Lee, *"Light Horse Harry."* Lee would become Marion's answer to the British Banastre Tarleton.

Lee had been with Greene at Guilford Courthouse in North Carolina and was able to provide Marion and his men details about that victory. The account had a very positive effect on the morale of Marion's men.

But Lee and Marion first had to resolve who was in charge. Greene had not been specific. Should it be Marion with his Brigadier General title in the militia or Lee as Lieutenant-Colonel in the Continental Army? After repelling Cornwallis in Charleston in 1776, Washington had elevated Marion's 2nd Regiment to the Continental Army but in the ensuing years Marion had operated as a militia leader often reporting to no one. Washington had never met Marion and, in fact, had never set foot in South Carolina.

Like Marion, Lee was highly accomplished but, unlike Marion, he was highly opinionated. But he soon developed an admiration for Marion and they worked out the relationship. Marion would be in charge.

Their first mission together was an attack on Georgetown. Georgetown was Marion's boyhood home, and it held sentimental value. It was also the top salt manufacturing location on the coast and salt was a highly prized commodity. In addition, with Charleston shut down, Georgetown was the export point of all the remaining rice plantations to the north and a transportation choke point for the Santee River.

Using a frowned upon strategy of sending men under a white flag into town to gain intelligence, Marion and Lee developed an amphibious attack plan. In what was supposed to be a coordinated attack by land and water, however, Lee and Marion arrived hours apart, losing the element of surprise. They managed to capture the British Commander and his two senior officers asleep in their beds but the rest of the garrison barricaded themselves in their fort. Without artillery or the means for an assault, Lee and Marion withdrew with only partially completed objectives. They sent their three prisoners off to the camp in Wilmington.

They returned to rebuild Snow's Island camp and found another letter had arrived from Greene. He had moved across the South Carolina border and, on January 17, at a place called Cowpens, had soundly defeated Marion's nemesis, Banastre Tarleton. Tarleton's 1,000-man force suffered 85% killed or wounded. In a one-hour engagement, Cornwallis had lost nearly one-quarter of his South Carolina Army. Tarleton himself had been wounded and had several fingers amputated. Perhaps the tide was turning.

Greene, however, had to head back north for supplies and was pursued by an enraged Cornwallis, all the way to Virginia. By April 1781, Cornwallis had given up the chase with his men exhausted and his supply lines stretched thin, all the way back to Charleston. Marion's control of the South Carolina bridges forced Cornwallis to give up the chase. The British General retreated to Wilmington, North Carolina, on the coast, to recover. Returning to his former headquarters in Charleston was out of the question. Cornwallis was done with South Carolina.

Greene and Marion continued to exchange notes but a new situation developed. There was a persistent rumor that a cease fire between Washington and Clinton might be negotiated. Under generally accepted rules at the time, the parties would agree to end hostilities with each side permitted to retain the land that they held. That would mean much of South Carolina, including Charleston, would remain British. Greene recognized this and increased the sense of urgency in his correspondence with Marion.

Marion and Greene discussed this in notes passed back and forth between them. Marion explained,

"Good, sir, you are not from the south so you do not understand the importance to this region of Georgetown and Charleston. The livelihood of the south flows across those two docks. If the British retain them, all we have fought for is for nought. You need to bring your forces down here and help me take back all of the Lowcountry."

Cornwallis also recognized this and had left a few thousand men in South Carolina, with most being in Charleston. To demonstrate the British ownership of all of South Carolina, he scattered his men across three dozen outposts around the state.

Greene received several more notes from Marion and Lee and soon realized he needed to reconsider his idea for a *"war of posts,"* as critical to regaining South Carolina. The idea had been discussed previously at high levels. Greene decided to act.

He assigned the South Carolina militia to the smaller posts and Greene's Continentals to the larger garrisons at Camden and at a place called Ninety-Six, the largest British station, far up in the upstate.

[Oller, 145]

Marion and Lee would be assigned the two most critical posts nearest to Charleston. Marion was given his first assignment in April 1781, take Fort Watson. It sat midway between Charleston and Camden and was now the major supply outpost for the British. Built by Marion's recent "Bridges Campaign" adversary, John Tadwell-Watson, and defended by 250 Redcoats, it sat high on a bluff and was shrouded in *abatis*, the French defensive styled walls. Earlier that year, South Carolina militia commander Colonel Sumter had failed miserably in an assault on Fort Watson, and Marion was skeptical that it could be taken. It would require a siege. Marion had participated in only one other siege, the disaster at Savannah in 1779. He was more effective at harassment. Sieges ended in suicide charges with enormous casualties, as he had seen in Savannah.

Watson was not actually at the fort at the time, but recovering in Georgetown, and The Swamp Fox wanted to capture him there. Light Horse Harry Lee, however, argued against this, reasoning that moving their force up to Georgetown again would put them too far from Greene. But Fort Watson had huge stores of something Marion desperately needed – ammunition. He reconsidered and moved his force to Fort Watson, arriving on April 15. Marion, at this point, had only 80 men and Lee had 300.

Marion arrived, surrounded the fort and demanded that the British commander, a British provincial officer, surrender, to which he replied with the expected response, *"If you want the fort, come and take it."*

Marion then began a siege. Fort Watson was small but strongly defended, sitting at the top of a 25-foot high former Indian Temple mound. The British had clear cut all the land surrounding it so there was no cover in which to hide. Three separate rows of abatis were built.

Neither side had artillery as both forces had discarded their field pieces in the recent Bridges campaign. The Americans cut off the fort's water supply and were running out of ammunition. They tunneled to within 100 yards of the walls. Cases of smallpox occurred in both camps as neither side had been inoculated. A few of Marion's men deserted. The siege dragged on and Marion was ready to quit.

Several days into it, one of Marion's officers approached him with an idea to build a tower from which they could fire down on the fort's inhabitants. It would have to be 30-feet tall. Grabbing axes from neighboring plantations, Marion's men constructed the tower at night, close to the fort. It was completed in late April and rolled into position. Marion positioned his skilled sharpshooters at the top and they began to rain precise fire down inside the fort inflicting heavy casualties. When Marion's men began to tear apart the abatis, the British commander raised the white flag. It was the first time since the fall of Charleston in 1780 that American forces had taken an entire British garrison.

Marion and Lee granted the British soldiers a parole to Charleston in exchange for American prisoners. Their Tory, fellow South Carolinians, who were captured, however, were treated as prisoners of war.

Lee was impressed with Marion's leadership, writing to Greene that he would like to remain under Marion's command.

The fall of Fort Watson was a critical loss to the British, not in terms of men and material, but in the geography of South Carolina and, more importantly, of the morale in Charleston. It was just a matter of time before the Swamp Fox would come calling.

[Oller, 147-150]

No sooner had Greene congratulated Marion on his success at Fort Watson, than he suffered a major loss at a place called Hobkirk's Hill, north of Camden. Another remote South Carolina battle site that has been lost in the history books, Hobkirk's Hill saw Greene's elite Maryland regiment drop their weapons and flee from an inferior British force. It was another loss in this war of success and failure.

Greene wrote to Marion, *"We fight, get beat, rise and fight again."*
[Crawford, 240-243]

But after the victory, the British commander at Camden made a hard decision. Starved for supplies, with no reinforcements coming and no support from the local population, he abandoned Camden, the site of Cornwallis' stunning victory over Gates just nine months earlier. He moved south towards Charleston as Marion eyed his next British outpost.

Chapter 42 ~ Fort Motte

With Fort Watson under Marion's control, his next assignment from Greene was Fort Motte, 30 miles upriver. It was the plantation home of Rebecca Motte, a widow and devout patriot who, throughout the war, used her slaves to pass intelligence to Marion and Moultrie. The Motte mansion in Charleston was the one that Cornwallis had selected as his personal headquarters when he was planning his operations in the South Carolina upstate.

Sitting in the middle of the state on the Congaree River, Motte Plantation was taken by the British after the fall of Charleston in 1780 and used as another major materials post between Camden and Charleston.

Marion and Lee arrived in early May 1781 with 400 men to find the former plantation was yet another citadel sitting on a 250-foot hill, surrounded by a ten-foot-high earthen wall. It was twice the size of Fort Watson. Two hundred British soldiers, Hessians and Tories, defended it. The commander was Lieutenant-Colonel Ferguson, the same man who passed up the opportunity to shoot Washington in the back at Brandywine.

A siege began with little progress being made and Marion was running out of time and patience. His attitude had turned melancholy. He had been more or less on his own for more than a year with no support, and with men coming and going from his command. Greene had not even managed to come down and meet Marion. He then received another note from Greene who was still up near Camden. Greene demanded that Marion provide him *"with 60 to 80 good dragoon horses."*

Marion exploded in anger and fired off a note to Greene stating that his men were weary and *"starting to drop away for lack of support."*

He went on to say, *"I acknowledge that you have repeatedly mentioned the want of dragoon horses, and wish that it had been in my power to furnish them, but it is not, nor has it ever been."*

He followed that up with an offer to resign, stating that he was considering traveling to Philadelphia to obtain reassignment from the Continental Congress.

Marion had clearly snapped under the strain of the war. Having been pursued for months by multiple British death squads, his camp at Snow's Island discovered and destroyed, his cousin recently murdered by Tarleton and with the almost total lack of support from Washington, he was ready to throw in the towel.

Greene was shocked at Marion's note. Never having met him, he could only imagine what pushed him over the edge. He made immediate plans to travel to Fort Motte and sent off a note apologizing to his subordinate.

Marion recovered from his fit and returned to the matter at hand. The siege was now in its seventh day with almost no sign of ending. Marion was unwilling to conduct a frontal assault up the hill which would certainly result in many casualties. He could not do that to these men who had been so loyal to him.

One of his men then came up with another idea – burn the British out. But in an odd twist of proper battlefield etiquette, permission needed to be obtained from Rebecca Motte, the lady of the plantation. After several hours of negotiation, she gave her permission and watched from a guest house on the plantation as American's launched flaming arrows onto the plantation house roof. Within minutes the roof was totally engaged and the British quickly surrendered, allowing the Americans to rush in and put out the fire, saving the plantation house.

In another awkward scene of 18th century battlefield protocol, the British commander Ferguson refused to surrender his sword to Marion who was officially a militia officer. Instead, he would only surrender to Lee who was Marion's subordinate but a Continental officer. This created some additional friction to Marion and Lee's relationship. In the end, the Tories in the fort surrendered to Marion's men who promptly hung three of them.

Greene arrived just as the British were surrendering. It was the first time he and Marion had met face to face. The two men saluted and shook hands with each sizing the other up. They both walked with a limp giving them something in common to talk about. For now, there was peace between them. The meeting was cordial but brief. They patched things up and Marion agreed to stay the course. Greene left immediately for the upstate.

[Crawford, 232-234]

One by one, the British posts were falling across South Carolina. The surrenders of Fort Watson and Fort Motte isolated Camden, the site of Cornwallis' crushing defeat of Gates just nine months earlier. The British had no choice but to abandon Camden and pull their beleaguered forces back to the safety of Charleston.

Chapter 43 ~ Georgetown

With Fort Watson and Fort Motte subdued and Marion's relationship with Greene somewhat repaired, The Swamp Fox turned his attention once again to his primary target in South Carolina – his boyhood home of Georgetown.

He and Lee had partial success there in January but the British garrison of 100 men was still in control.

He wrote to Greene on May 19, "*I beg leave to go and reduce that place.*"

[Oller, 161]

Marion was resting his men at Peyre's Plantation, his new camp on the Santee River, close to his boyhood home of Belle Isle. Peyre's was a lot like his former secluded camp of Snow's Island that Cornwallis had found and destroyed. This new camp was deep in the forest and protected by creeks and swamps.

Greene had other ideas, however. There was one large remaining British garrison at a place called Ninety-Six in Greenwood County northwest of Columbia. It was nearly 200 miles from the Lowcountry where Marion was camped. Ninety-Six was defended by more than 500 Redcoats and was the last remaining upstate outpost. Greene did not want Marion that far away if he needed him in a siege at Ninety-Six.

Greene then did something that infuriated Marion once again. He reaffirmed Thomas Sumter as head of the South Carolina militia, meaning that Marion reported to him. He sent Marion a note to "*...await Sumter's orders.*"

Sumter, the famous "Gamecock," had a checkered history of success and failure and had been operating somewhat independently throughout the state. He had previously been a Continental officer under Greene but resigned his commission two years earlier. When the British torched his plantation home and used it as a prisoner of war camp, he was enraged and took up arms again. Sumter and his men had been ravaging the countryside using plunder as motivation. Marion had no respect for him.

Marion took advantage of the delays in communications with Greene and Sumter and immediately set out for Georgetown. He was not about to ask for permission from his commanding officer.

He arrived at Georgetown without any artillery, not wanting to be delayed. The British commander quickly saw that his position was being surrounded. Marion then resorted to subterfuge, as he had in the past. His men cut down several pine trees, skinned the bark off of them and tarred them black to resemble cannons, rolling them into position and pointed at the British.

He sent a note to the Redcoat commander, a loyalist named Robert Gray, "*Abandon your position or suffer our cannon assault. We will permit you to leave on your ships at Georgetown Front Street.*"

Marion did not have a single cannon but Gray abandoned his position, boarded his ships in Georgetown, and sailed out to Winyah Bay heading for the safety of Charleston.

Marion had taken Georgetown without a shot being fired.

Chapter 44 ~ Ninety-Six

Sumter had nothing to say to Marion but tried to take credit for the Georgetown success with Greene. Greene then directed that Marion move his force to Moncks Corner and Sumter to Dorchester, the last two remaining outposts protecting Charleston.

It was reported that 2,000 more British soldiers, men from Ireland, had arrived in Charleston and would be led by Lieutenant Colonel Francis Rawdon. Rawdon had been operating in South Carolina for more than two years but, with Cornwallis and Tarleton now in Virginia, he was the senior British officer in the south.

Upon taking command, Rawdon had ordered the commander of Ninety-Six to abandon it but Greene's scouts intercepted the British courier. The message was encoded and could not be interpreted by the rebels. Had it been delivered the ensuing battle would have never happened.

Greene arrived from the long march from the Low Country, rested for two days and then commenced a classic siege on at the town of Ninety-Six in Greenwood County. It did not go well. The area surrounding it was heavily loyalist and the fort itself was heavily defended with a star formation, eight pointed sets of walls.

Greene tried Marion's successful tactics from Watson and Motte but the British thwarted him. Greene finally tried a frontal assault and suffered massive casualties. He had no choice but to admit defeat and withdraw.

Rawdon came out from Charleston and pursued Greene in his

retreat, but the 100-degree South Carolina summer overcame his Irish soldiers. Fifty died of heatstroke and he returned to the Ninety-Six fort to rest and recuperate from the heat.

But Rawdon quickly realized the reality of the situation. With all the other South Carolina outposts now controlled by the Americans, he had no ability to supply the Ninety-Six garrison. He decided to abandon it in July and moved his forces to Orangeburg.

Greene considered assaulting Rawdon at Orangeburg and called Marion up to assist. But Greene's soldiers, mostly from Virginia, were exhausted and starving. Accustomed to beef, corn and wheat bread, they could not tolerate the South Carolina rice and resorted to eating frogs and alligators. Greene took his men to the cooler hills of Santee for the rest of the summer.

But one thing was certain. The major outpost of Ninety-Six was in American hands. Greene had won by losing.

South Carolina was slowly but surely falling under Marion's control. But where was Washington and the French?

Chapter 45 ~ John Laurens in Paris

In the spring of 1781, while Francis Marion was harassing various British posts in South Carolina and Lafayette was pursuing Cornwallis and Arnold across Virginia, John Laurens was in Paris working to secure the materials, supplies, munitions and, most importantly, money to allow Washington to continue the war. King Louis XVI had sent his Navy and troops across the Atlantic the previous summer but they were inactive, waiting for supplies to fight. Ministers in the French palace were impatient, reluctant to expend any more resources on this American expedition and were considering recalling their Army and Navy. The powerful French foreign minister, Charles Gravier, Comte de Vergennes, was opposed to sending more aid. The ultimate decision, however, was with King Louis.

John Laurens and Ben Franklin quickly struck up a friendship despite their ages and contrasting styles. Thomas Paine, the much-respected diplomat and orator, had accompanied Laurens on the trip but, unable to speak French, he was limited in his effectiveness, and Franklin and Laurens excluded him from several key conversations.

Franklin's style was one of "slow and steady." He did not have the advantage of Laurens' personal experiences and the desperation felt in Philadelphia.

John Laurens was much more impatient. He was approaching his 27th birthday and had been sent by Washington with the message *"time is running out."* He had been in Paris for several months and in the King's presence at Court but unable to secure a private audience. Laurens, wounded in battle, had seen friends die and his homeland destroyed. He knew in detail Washington's precarious situation and was impatient to say the least.

One day, he said to Franklin, "If only I could get to him. I think I can appeal to his sense of history and democracy. But, Mr. Franklin, we are not making progress and time is running out."

Franklin looked up from his newspaper, peering over the top of his glasses and nodded in assent but said nothing.

Laurens had been an immediate sensation when he arrived in the court of King Louis. This 26-year-old son of the American President of Congress and battlefield hero spoke fluent French from his years of schooling in Paris and was quickly known as a passionate spokesman for American independence. But weeks passed with no progress as Laurens and Franklin tried to wind their way through the French bureaucracy.

The French people looked at the American struggle against the British as a sort of theater, designed for their amusement. Battles were won, battles were lost, British generals replaced, American heroes like Lafayette, Laurens, and Marion were in the newspapers in Paris frequently. It made for entertaining reading and lively conversation at dinner parties.

Franklin was playing the long game in Paris and, quite frankly, was enjoying the assignment. He had struck up an intimate relationship with a French countess and was enjoying his celebrity, first as the *"inventor of electricity"* and later as a witty, erudite and oft-quoted American.

Laurens continued, "I think we need to force our hand. Lafayette made our case when he was here last year but, since then, all the King has heard are reasons why not to help us."

Franklin listened and tried to calm his young companion down but Laurens was insistent. By the end of the night, after several glasses of wine, it was agreed that the two of them would go to the court the next morning, breaking protocol, and demand to see the King.

The next day, they arrived at the Palace of Versailles unannounced, stating that they were Americans on an urgent mission. Guards outside recognized Franklin by sight and allowed them to pass. When they approached the Grand Salon, however, their way was blocked.

John Laurens was not to be denied. He could not give up. They barged through the door to the Great Hall to the gasp of the court attendants. Armed guards restrained them but King Louis, hearing the commotion and recognizing Franklin, told the Salon guards to stand back.

The opulence of the French Court was overwhelming. Tall windows framed by velvet curtains let in rays of soft morning light, illuminating gilded walls and intricately detailed tapestries. The air was rich with the scent of fresh flowers and the faint murmur of courtiers could be heard in the distance. Franklin stepped aside and allowed his young countryman to enter ahead of him. Another of the court's many guards stepped in front of John blocking his path on the red velvet carpet up to the throne.

King Louis looked up from a scroll he was reading and immediately recognized the young American. He raised his right hand with the palm facing up and rolled his fingers indicating he should approach. The guard stood aside.

At the foot of the throne stood John Laurens, wearing a finely tailored military uniform, his face calm but resolute. He slowly bowed from the waist. The next few minutes could turn the tide of the war for American independence.

Opposite John, up a few steps, seated in an ornately carved chair, sat King Louis XVI of France. The king, dressed in lavish silks and brocade, wore a neutral expression, though his eyes betrayed a cautious interest. Beside him, a few French ministers and advisers stood quietly, observing Laurens with measured glances.

King Louis was fascinated with John Laurens, as he had never met an American his own age. He had spoken at length on previous occasions with Lafayette, but he was a Frenchman. As it turned out, the king and John Laurens were both born in 1754, both approaching their 27th birthdays. King Louis nodded to John, indicating that he should begin.

"Your Majesty, I come on behalf of General Washington and the Continental Congress to ask for your continued support in our struggle for liberty."

"Monsieur Laurens, your young nation has already benefited from France's generosity. We have sent troops, ships, and supplies. What more do you seek?"

Laurens took a half step forward causing the guards to react. The young king raised his hand once again and they backed away. Laurens continued. What he said in the next few minutes would determine the fate of his fledgling country.

"I understand the sacrifices France has made, Your Majesty, and they are appreciated beyond measure. But I speak to you now not just as an American envoy but as a soldier who has fought in this war and witnessed its hardships firsthand."

Laurens had studied debate at college in both London and France, thinking of a career as a lawyer, arguing in court. He hesitated for a beat, as if choosing his next words carefully.

"The British forces remain powerful. Our soldiers are brave but courage alone cannot win battles. We are in desperate need of further financial support—loans to fund the war effort and provisions to sustain our troops through this final push."

The room fell silent for a moment as Laurens let his words sink in. The king's advisers behind him exchanged brief, unreadable glances.

The king raised one eyebrow, "And what guarantees does your Congress offer, Monsieur Laurens? France has its own financial troubles and this war has not come without cost."

John Laurens nodded in acknowledgment, "It is true, Your Majesty, that we cannot offer immediate repayment. But this is no ordinary conflict. What we fight for is not just the independence of one nation but the hope of liberty for all people. If we succeed, it will shift the balance of power away from Britain, your greatest rival."

He paused, his eyes bright with conviction. He could see those words hit home with the king.

"America will never forget France's role in this victory. When peace is won, we will work tirelessly to repay our debts."

There was a murmur from the king's ministers. The weight of Laurens' words lingered in the air, a promise of future alliances and shared interests. The king sat back, contemplating this young American.

Louis stood up, causing everyone in the Grand Salon to take notice, "Walk with me, Mr. Laurens."

With that, the king descended from his throne and out a side door with John Laurens one half-step behind.

They proceeded into the garden, just behind the palace and, when court attendants and guards tried to follow, King Louis waved them away.

They strolled through endless rose gardens and then behind a wall of finely manicured evergreens. Louis changed the subject and began to speak of his wife and family. They walked for several minutes talking and gesturing about their young lives and their families. Louis was even more fascinated with John when they both began to speak in Latin, but John's command of that ancient language was much better than the King's.

The subject changed back to the matter at hand.

"You speak of ideals, Monsieur Laurens. But ideals do not win wars, nor pay for them." The king stopped walking and faced John Laurens.

This was Laurens' chance. The king was signaling he wanted to help but money was the issue. This was no longer about politics. He had a chance to appeal to the young king's legacy.

"Your Majesty, I speak to you as a son speaks to a father. I have seen men starve, freeze, and fight with nothing but hope to sustain them. And yet, they keep fighting."

Here, he held a long pause, "We are so close to victory, but we are stretched to our limits. If you help us now—if you give us the resources we need—then history will remember France as the true champion of liberty."

For the first time, King Louis' stern expression softened and he regarded Laurens with something like admiration. Laurens had spoken not just to the political realities of war but to the king's desire for a legacy, for France to be seen as a nation of greatness and virtue.

"You ask much, Monsieur Laurens. But I see the fire in your eyes—the same fire that burns in your General Washington and in my dear Lafayette."

He paused for a long minute, "Very well. I will provide additional funds and supplies. Not just for your war but for the principles you defend."

Laurens felt a surge of relief and pride but he maintained his composure, bowing deeply.

"Your Majesty, you have not only secured the friendship of a nation, but the gratitude of every man, woman, and child who longs to breathe free."

"We shall see, Monsieur Laurens. We shall see. I will speak to Vergennes."

John Laurens bowed, "Vive la France."

To which the King replied, "Vive l'Amérique."

Two months later, in August 1781, as Cornwallis was settling into Yorktown, John Laurens and Thomas Paine left France on two ships containing arms, munitions, supplies and a chest with six million French livres, a personal gift from the King of France. The voyage, fortunately, was uneventful.

When they arrived in America, they were shocked at what they found. The American troops were mutinying!

Chapter 46 ~ The Yorktown Decision

As spring turned to summer in 1781 and negotiations with the French were bogged down, Washington desired to attack Clinton in New York, avenging his ignominious defeat there five years earlier. But the French commander, Rochambeau, had other ideas. He had received orders from Paris to work with Washington to end the war but he wanted to do this in a way that projected his glory, not Washington's.

Rochambeau had 8,000 French troops under his command in addition to his powerful fleet under Admiral DeGrasse. But Clinton in New York was reported to have nearly 17,000 well-rested British soldiers. Cornwallis, however, down in Virginia was showing definite signs of weakness with repeated losses in South Carolina to an American backwoods military leader named Marion. Constant communications from Lafayette confirmed Cornwallis' precarious situation. The British general in charge of the *Southern Strategy* had left garrisons in Charleston and Savannah but his main body was now near the Chesapeake Bay. In August, Cornwallis, under orders from Clinton, moved the main body of his forces to the city of Yorktown, high on a bluff.

From Yorktown, Cornwallis could ride out the winter waiting for reinforcements from New York.

Rochambeau decided Cornwallis was the easier opponent. But time was not on their side. Fall was approaching, and it would take months to move the Army and Navy to Virginia.

Lafayette, still in Virginia, took notice of the British Army movements and sent notes to Washington and Rochambeau urging them to surround Cornwallis in Yorktown.

Washington, negotiating with Rochambeau from a position of weakness, had to accede to the Yorktown plan. Meetings were held in Hartford in July and August, and the decision was made. Forces from both armies would gather near Washington's camp in Morristown, New Jersey, and march south to Virginia. The French Navy would seal off the Yorktown River, giving Cornwallis no avenue of escape.

On August 17, DeGrasse was informed by Rochambeau and Washington of the new destination – Yorktown. He was ordered to position his Navy to secure the river and expect an assault from the British Navy.

But Washington and Rochambeau had other issues. Could they maintain the element of surprise with Clinton's spies watching their every move? Given advance warning, Clinton could reposition his forces from New York to Yorktown. Once again, the slow methodical movement of armies and navies in the 1700s worked to Washington's advantage.

In early September, with thousands of men now camped in and around Morristown, Washington held a meeting in nearby Chatham. Knowing that Clinton was watching their every move, they needed a diversion. Washington held a secret meeting with only his senior officers and aides. The flaps on the command tent were sealed with Washington's personal bodyguards outside. Alexander Hamilton was in attendance. Laurens was not yet back from Paris, and Lafayette and Samuel Huger were still monitoring Cornwallis in Virginia.

"Gentlemen, we leave in one week. Nobody outside this room is to know our plan until the day before. In the meantime, I have an idea. A ruse. A deception. I want bread ovens built here in

Chatham. The French Army must have its bread. Everyone knows that. We will provide the bricks, the French will provide the labor and we will accumulate firewood to heat the ovens. Once the presence of these ovens is noticed by our Tory friends, they will hopefully conclude that we are settling in for the assault on New York."

Within a few days, the smell of French bread cooking wafted across the village and the British spies took note. It was quickly reported to Clinton. There could be only one conclusion, the French were settling in for a siege of New York. This bread would fill their stomachs. Clinton quickly recalled several regiments from Westchester County and Long Island. There was no doubt. The Americans and their French partners would begin assaulting New York.

Washington's ruse worked.

One week later, at 4 AM, the American and French soldiers were awakened and began to march south. At first, they thought they were being positioned along the New Jersey coast for the assault. When they reached Trenton and Philadelphia, a different conclusion was apparent. They were heading south, but where? They were nearing Maryland when word was finally reported to Clinton. He had been duped. All he could do was quickly outfit a small fleet south to Yorktown and hope it arrived before the Americans.

The British fleet left New York in mid-September under Admiral Thomas Graves and when they arrived at the mouth of the Chesapeake, the French Admiral DeGrasse was waiting for them. In what was later called The Battle of The Virginia Capes, both forces lined up taking the classic sea battle position. The French, however, had the upper hand positioning themselves upwind with a superior firepower. Both sides suffered losses but the damage the British sustained was devastating.

Graves withdrew and sailed north to face the wrath of Clinton.

Control of the Chesapeake and the York River was in the hands of the French.

Chapter 47 ~ September, 1781

John Laurens and Thomas Paine arrived in Philadelphia in early September to find that Washington had already left for Yorktown. After ensuring their valuable cargo made its way to Congress and the Continental Army supply chain, Laurens set out to catch up with Washington. He caught up with the American Army in Maryland and was shocked at what he found.

Large numbers of Continental soldiers had laid down their arms, refusing to go any farther until they were paid and adequately clothed. In Elkton, Maryland, hundreds of them were, in effect, on strike. The mood was ugly, and Washington was at his wit's end. He needed these men to fight alongside the French so he was reluctant to punish them. After all, what they were demanding was reasonable. The French soldiers in the adjacent camps, well fed and well paid, looked on with amusement.

John caught up with Washington at his command tent. The general had his typical frown but John was beaming. He quickly explained his successful mission to Paris and agreed to meet with the company commanders. It took a few days but the funds from Congress made their way to the Continental Army. Lines formed in front of the paymasters' tents and men emerged, smiling. Uniforms, weapons and food then began to flow, further alleviating the tension.

Laurens met with Washington and Hamilton soon after the crisis had passed. Lafayette and Huger were still down in Virginia awaiting their army's arrival. The mood was markedly improved. Hamilton, always the voice of reason, spoke first.

"General, the crisis has passed. We need to move quickly. We all know winter is approaching. We can hold DeGrasse in position only so long. My information is that he wants to leave now before storms arrive."

It was Laurens turn to speak.

"Sir, it seems that we are getting back to the matter at hand. The French have moved down the peninsula and the French admiral has dispatched boats to escort our men down the Chesapeake Bay. But there is one additional matter I wish to discuss with you."

Washington snuck a look at Hamilton, knowing that these two aides had already collaborated on what was coming next.

"Well, Colonel, what is it?"

Laurens was now technically a civilian due to his French parole agreement but Washington still referred to him with his former military rank.

"I wish to get back in uniform with a regimental command, sir."

The general frowned, waving his hand at the suggestion.

"You know the terms of your release from Cornwallis prohibit you from fighting, do you not?"

"Of course, sir, but you know full well men like Benedict Arnold have totally disrespected any prior agreements."

"I have a more important, less glorious role for you, Colonel. I need to utilize your relationship with King Louis along with your command of French in our negotiations with DeGrasse and Rochambeau. Neither of them has any English-speaking aides, and I don't want anything confused or miscommunicated in these coming days. There is too much at stake."

"But sir ..."

"That is all, Colonel. Start by drafting a note to DeGrasse asking for the positioning of his gunboats once we begin our assault. He is considering leaving only two gunboats on the river to block Cornwallis' escape and that is insufficient. I'm counting on you, John, to convince him we need his entire fleet."

Washington did not often speak to his young aides using their first names. Laurens, Hamilton, and Lafayette were like sons to him and everyone knew it. This now was a personal request from the Commander in Chief. John could not argue anymore.

Washington then turned to Hamilton.

"We need to discuss the movement of our munitions and cannons down from Philadelphia. I need to know where they are and when they will arrive."

With that, he waved his hand at the two aides. They knew from their years with him that this meeting was over.

Chapter 48 ~ Yorktown, October 1781

Yorktown, Virginia, in 1781 was a bustling little river town sitting high on a cliff overlooking the York River inside of Chesapeake Bay. Gloucester Point jutted out from the opposite side of the river making it an effective choke point for access to the interior of Virginia.

A former tobacco trading post, it was shocked into awareness in August 1781 with the arrival of thousands of British soldiers under General Cornwallis. They took over every inn, farm and even barns and their tent camps were everywhere. They began constructing large circular mounds to the amazement of the residents. These would be the infamous redoubts, so common in siege warfare in Europe. The redoubts were inter-connected by huge earthen walls constructed by the soldiers and the local workers. It circled around the small village offering protection from a land-based assault.

Once the British Navy withdrew back to New York, Lafayette began meetings with DeGrasse on transporting the approaching French and American troops downriver towards Yorktown. Lafayette had also been given a firm order from Washington.

"Hold the British in Virginia at all costs."

Cornwallis was apparently oblivious to the storm that was coming toward him. He was settling in for the winter.

On September 28, the combined French and American forces drew to within a few miles of Yorktown, and the British welcomed them with a fierce artillery bombardment.

Lafayette soon arrived with Huger and nearly 2,000 more men. Washington and Rochambeau's combined forces now numbered nearly 20,000.

Optimism in the American camp had never been higher.

The siege process began on October 1 when American sappers began digging trenches parallel to the ones the British had dug. Several hundred Americans began cutting down trees.

Both sides quickly began to dig in as the American artillery, which had just arrived, was moved into position.

On October 9, Washington symbolically *"put the match to the first gun"* with Rochambeau looking on.

[Crawford, 293-295]

For several days, the cannon fire from both sides continued and the citizens of Yorktown paid a terrible price. With their homes destroyed, they fled down the hill to the safety of the river waterfront, with no place else to go.

But Cornwallis was also trapped with no avenue of escape. He was surrounded on three sides, with his back to a river that was now controlled by the French Navy. Cornwallis himself was even bombed out of the Governor's house, where he had established his headquarters, and was wounded.

Cornwallis then decided he would try to escape. He had a small boat brought to the dock, down the hill from Yorktown, thinking he could elude the French river patrols and make it across to Gloucester Point. A violent storm came up and he had to return up the hill.

When Washington learned of that, he said to Hamilton, *"Even providence is on our side now."*

Daily meetings with Rochambeau were held, with Lafayette and Laurens translating.

A smallpox epidemic was arising within the Yorktown city walls and, in another desperate move, Cornwallis released infected plantation slaves he had taken from Jefferson, sending them into the American Army camp. They were interrogated and quickly isolated.

During this time, John Laurens had been relegated to writing and translating the communications from Washington to Rochambeau, and he was not happy about it. Once again, however, fate intervened on his behalf.

Early one morning, an American colonel, Alexander Scammell, was captured by the British while conducting reconnaissance on their positions. John Laurens saw his opportunity. Washington relented and gave him command of Scammell's battalion. One last time, Washington's "*Three Sons*" would have battlefield commands together.

Washington and Rochambeau conferred with their battle commanders. Time was running out for Washington. The French Admiral DeGrasse was, once again, threatening to withdraw to the Caribbean before winter set in. If that happened, Cornwallis would be able to escape down the Yorktown River. With Laurens and Lafayette translating, a plan emerged for the final stage of the siege.

An assault on the two main redoubts that Cornwallis had built, closest to the city, was needed. After several hours of negotiation, agreement was reached. Redoubt #9, on the left, would be the responsibility of the French soldiers. Redoubt #10, on the right, larger and more heavily defended, fell to the Continentals. Alexander Hamilton, at long last in a field command, and Lafayette, along with Samuel Huger's company, would lead the midnight assault. John Laurens with 80 men was assigned to circle around and attack the city from the rear. They would all be in the vanguard of the assault.

When they received their assignments, Lafayette, Laurens, and Hamilton all stood facing each other. Samuel Huger was also there, but off to the side, observing. They had been through much in these last four years. They were still young men but suddenly felt very old. None wanted to show his fear but assaulting a heavily fortified British position at night would certainly result in heavy casualties. They saluted and shook hands. Pulling on their tri-cornered hats, they went to their assignments.

The men were given their orders and they gathered in the trenches, making last minute preparations and saying silent payers.

Hamilton entrusted the first wave of his company to that tall young lieutenant, Nate Muchmore, the former writer for the Chatham *Jersey Journal*. Nate had impressed Hamilton from the first time they met with his heroics at the Battle of Springfield. He would now entrust him with this important command. Nate and his men would be among the first to approach Redoubt #10.

On Hamilton's right flank were Lafayette and his Maryland men. Given his rank now as brigadier-general, he was not expected to cross the field with his men. He selected the company under Samuel Huger for his first wave. Lafayette and Samuel had been together now for more than five long years, since that day he stepped onto the Huger's North Island dock.

Laurens, far to the right, commanded a company of men he did not know. But his reputation as a fearless leader preceded him and they trusted each other. They had no choice.

Casualties were expected to be high and the two companies under Muchmore and Huger would likely make the first contact with the British in this struggle.

Far to the left were the French companies, immaculately dressed in their uniforms.

Hamilton met with his officers and gave them their final instructions. Lafayette did the same a few hundred yards down the trench.

"When the cannon fire stops, we go!"

Chapter 49 ~ Redoubt #10

Laurens crept out with his men around the far-right flank, circling wide around the city as the American cannon fire died down.

It was time to go. When the American cannons finally silenced, that was the signal that the assault was about to commence. Up over the trench walls the Americans went in the darkness. Each man carried a musket with a bayonet fixed. The first wave had no ammunition. This was hoped to be a surprise and the risk of an accidental round going off was too high. The second wave, right behind the first, would each have one round loaded in their musket. There would be no time to stop and reload. This would be close quarters, hand-to-hand fighting.

To their left, hundreds of French soldiers did the same. Creeping low in the darkness.

Samuel motioned to his men and up they went, crouching low. There was nothing to hide behind. The British had cleared the field for several hundred yards.

The battlefield was eerily silent.

Sappers followed behind with special tools to tear apart the redoubt abatis. The first hundred yards were uneventful. The silhouettes of the redoubts ahead came into view.

With the silencing of the American cannons, the British were on the alert. The soldiers within the redoubts took their positions, guns at the ready.

Then the British launched flares high into the air, exposing the hundreds of men coming up the hill. The French were characteristically flying their colors, staying in a tight formation. Samuel looked to his right and could see Nate Muchmore and the three dozen Chatham boys. He turned to look at his men, grim faced at what was about to happen. When the flares reached their maximum height, the British guns exploded and both French and American boys began dropping to the ground, screaming out in pain. Blue smoke from the British musket fire drifted across the landscape, blocking their vision.

Samuel pressed on with two of his men falling. Then a third, and a fourth. At 40 yards, he gave the order, and his men began to run towards the redoubt.

The redoubts consisted of a trench, beyond which was a mound about 12-feet high and one hundred yards long. Halfway up were pine trees that had been cut, stripped and pointed outwards to stop anyone from climbing.

Redoubt #10 at Yorktown, 2024.

Once at the base, Samuel signaled for the sappers to move forward. Several of them were also ravaged by the British fire but now they were reloading. Other Americans grabbed their tools and began disassembling the redoubt walls. Within a few minutes, narrow paths up to the top of the redoubt were cleared. But there were many casualties.

Hamilton's companies under Lieutenant Muchmore were doing the same on the other side of the redoubt. His face was bloody from a bullet that had grazed him.

British soldiers would appear at the top, fire, and then disappear.

Then all at once, the Americans ascended the redoubt, shouting and screaming as they climbed. Several more boys were wounded and fell to the side. But they pushed forward. They went up and over into the British stronghold. Americans poured in from several directions. It was a scene of utter chaos.

While this was happening, John Laurens approached one of the city's rear gates and, surprisingly, found it lightly guarded. His men quickly disposed of the guards and ran inside, fanning out through two streets. Redcoats were running towards them, unarmed, having fled from the frontal assault on the redoubts. Laurens' men took several prisoners.

Back inside the redoubt, there was a lot of confusion with men screaming and fighting with anything they could get their hands on. Hamilton arrived and was surprised at how few of the enemy were actually standing their ground. Most of the Hessian defenders had turned and run back into the city once the Americans breached the walls. The second wave of Americans then arrived, firing as they entered.

The same thing was occurring with the French in Redoubt #9. In fact, they raised the French flag in victory before the Americans could do the same. That honor fell to Hamilton's Lieutenant Nate Muchmore.

And then it was over. The guns silenced, the men rested, prisoners were lined up and searched. British muskets were accumulated in a pile. The second and third waves streamed in, relieving the first waves. The British cannons were turned and pointed at the city.

Some men broke down as the dead and wounded were laid out and counted. Dozens of men lie dead, too many to count. Many were wounded, and American doctors circulated among them. A steady stream of stretchers was bringing men back to the American lines.

Dawn broke over Yorktown. Around 10 AM, a 14-year-old British drummer emerged with a British officer behind him, waving a white handkerchief. With sporadic gunfire still going on, the Americans nearly shot him. Lafayette spotted him and ordered a cease fire.

The Redcoat officer was blindfolded and escorted across the field to Washington and Rochambeau's command tent. Cornwallis was asking for a 24-hour cessation in fighting so that "*settlement terms are negotiated in a meeting at Mr. Moore's house.*" Among Cornwallis' requests was that his men be allowed to retain their weapons and march out with their colors flying. Notes were exchanged that day and Washington gave Cornwallis only two hours.

At 4:30 that day, Cornwallis sent a note, "*The basis of my proposals will be that the garrisons of York and Gloucester shall be prisoners of war with the customary honours. The British soldiers shall be sent to Britain and the Germans to Germany, under engagement not to serve against France or America or their Allies ...*"

[Greene, 282-285]

Washington and Rochambeau were in no mood to negotiate.

Washington appointed John Laurens to handle the negotiations, with very specific instructions. Rochambeau assigned Jean de Noailles, Lafayette's father-in-law, to represent the French.

The next day, as the British were scuttling their ships in York-town harbor, the meeting was held.

Washington was willing to be generous, except on one point. Given how the British had humiliated General Lincoln's men in Charleston in 1780, Cornwallis' men would be treated the same. Cornwallis then requested that he be allowed to hand his sword directly to Washington in another sign of honor and respect. Washington again refused, instructing the British general to submit to General Lincoln, the American general whom Cornwallis had defeated at Charleston.

Laurens and the French field commander crossed the field with the young British bugler boy holding the white flag. Walking through rows of scowling British soldiers, they were escorted to Cornwallis' tent.

The delicious irony of the moment was not lost on John Laurens.

Cornwallis, however, did not attend, sending word that he was ill. Two of his senior officers stood in for him – Major Alexander Ross and Lieutenant Colonel Thomas Dundas.

Laurens, now in diplomat mode, opened the discussion.

"Sirs, we have not met but I have met your commanding officer, under much different circumstances. It is regrettable that he could not attend today."

Laurens tried, unsuccessfully, to suppress a smile looking at his French partner.

"Let me introduce my colleague and partner Monsieur le Duc de Noailles, representing General Rochambeau."

Noailles nodded, removing his hat.

Twenty-six-year-old John Laurens paused for a long minute, taking in the reversal of fortune for his British adversary. He could not help but wonder what would happen to Cornwallis back in London after this defeat. But he thought of the carnage Cornwallis had inflicted on his home state, not to mention the imprisonment of his father.

Major Ross started to speak but Laurens did not want to hear what he had to say.

"Your men will march out at 10 AM tomorrow in their uniforms with their colors stored away and will stack their arms. Officers and enlisted men will be separated and processed according to custom. They will all be marched to a camp we have set up where they will be fed and their wounds treated by American doctors."

He let that sink in for a minute. Washington was not giving them the respect of flying their colors, a deep European tradition.

"General Benjamin Lincoln, who I think you know …"

He paused and let that sink in. "… will accept your sword as a sign of surrender. You and your men are now our prisoners. The war is over for you, sirs. Good day to you."

With that, he and Noailles stood, saluted and exited the tent.

The next morning, the French and Americans lined up facing each other as the British marched out, stacked their arms and were led away. The French stood silently but the American boys could not resist hooting and howling at the Redcoats. Cornwallis feigned illness and did not show up as his men marched silently out of Yorktown into American prison camps. Cornwallis was later taken into custody. In the ultimate irony, he would be exchanged in a few months for John Laurens' father, Henry Laurens.

After the British had been marched off, the men all returned to their camps. The march back north would be a triumphant one.

Washington's "three sons" heartily congratulated the men who had been with them that previous night and several were awarded medals by Washington. Lafayette was given the honor of pinning the medals on the bravest, kissing each heartily on both cheeks.

That night, Washington and Rochambeau split a bottle of fine

French wine to celebrate. With Cornwallis and his 7,000 Redcoats removed from the war, surely the English would finally admit defeat.

Hamilton, Lafayette, and Laurens, along with Samuel Huger, all sat down to have dinner together around a warm campfire. The October evenings were starting to get chilly now in Virginia and the warmth from the fire felt good.

These four men, still in their mid-twenties, had already experienced in life what few men ever do. They had survived a brutal war with a front row seat to the decisions that would shape the United States of America.

Washington's attendants brought them plates of stew prepared for Washington and his generals. There was plenty to go around. Lafayette produced two bottles of wine he had obtained from the French camp and poured it into tin cups for his comrades.

These young men, who had been through so much together in the last four years, looked at each other, and it suddenly occurred to them that they might not have another moment like this. Samuel thought back to that time years earlier when Lafayette and DeKalb stepped onto the Huger dock on North Island. It seemed like yesterday.

Suddenly they were all very weary – of the stress, the anguish, the disease, the death, and destruction. They had all witnessed horrible things, things they would not want to talk about in the coming years.

Samuel said what they were all thinking.

"Hopefully, this is the end of it. Clinton must surely see now he cannot prevail, and this is over. I suspect we will soon go our separate ways. Gilbert, what are your plans?"

Lafayette cocked his head and thought for a second.

"Messieurs, you all know of my strong desire to return to my home country and rejoin my wife and children. Adrienne has been very patient with me all these years. I want to see my children, very badly."

John Laurens spoke next.

"I will be leaving soon for South Carolina. With my father still in the Tower of London, I am the head of our family now and I must see what I can do to restore my family's businesses. This war has destroyed much of what my father built in Charleston. When I was imprisoned in our family home, I was able to see the full extent of the damage. Once I get settled, I will send for Matilda in London. I don't think my letters to her have reached her during all this time, so I pray she and my daughter are well. I also think that the Tories back home may not lay down their arms, and I will see what I can do to assist Moultrie and Greene in restoring order to my state. There are many unknowns."

It was Hamilton's turn to speak.

"We may have defeated the British Army and Navy, but I don't think we have a viable country yet. The Congress remains bitterly divided and we will need a central government like what you have in France … without a king, of course."

They all laughed at that, and Lafayette bowed to their amusement.

"I don't know what role Washington wishes to play going forward but I will stay to assist him. Elizabeth and I will move to wherever Washington needs me."

Samuel then stood and looked at all of them.

"Gentlemen, serving you these past four years has been the greatest honor of my life. You have treated me with grace, dignity, and respect, trusting me with some of our most important decisions. I will return to South Carolina and serve with John until he no longer needs me. The Huger family, like many, has lost much in this conflict and I don't honestly know if it can be rebuilt. But South Carolina is my home and that is where I must go."

Hamilton then spoke.

"Well said, Palmetto Patriot, well said."

By now it was late, and the day had been very long. They each shook hands and hugged, not knowing what would come next. They toasted each other one last time and retired to their tents, exhausted to the core. It would be the last time they were all together.

For one of them, however, time was running very short.

Chapter 50 ~ The Yorktown Myth

With the surrender of Cornwallis in October 1781, there was a sense among many that the war was over. Or was it?

After all, a senior British general, responsible for so much American death and destruction, had surrendered his entire garrison of 7,000 men. But the fact remained that Henry Clinton still had 17,000 troops in New York. Charleston was still in British hands, defended by several thousand more Redcoats. Despite Greene and Marion's successes in South Carolina, dozens of other small outposts were manned by determined Redcoats. Not to mention the pockets of Loyalist citizens poised for retribution.

Viewed in perspective, Cornwallis' defeat at Yorktown was equivalent to the American's defeat in Charleston two years earlier and yet the Americans fought on. The British might be expected to do the same.

It took nearly a month for word of the Americans' victory at Yorktown to reach London. For many Englishmen, that was the last straw. Members of Parliament were fed up.

But King George III wrote to Parliament, "*I have no doubts, when men are a little recovered from the shock felt by the bad news, they will find the necessity of carrying on the war.*"

Parliament, however, would have none of it. They were done. This war was bankrupting the country.

[Crawford, 99]

General Greene and Colonel Marion in South Carolina got the news from Yorktown on October 27. In that same communication from Washington was the warning that Clinton could be expected to send thousands more Redcoats to South Carolina.

Greene famously replied, "*We cannot march without shoes, and we cannot fight without ammunition.*"

Greene's spirits were buoyed by the arrival of his young wife from Philadelphia. Reluctantly separated from her husband when Washington assigned him to replace Gates, Caty Greene insisted on joining him. She stopped at Kiawah Island on the trip south to visit and care for wounded Americans who were convalescing.

Greene and Marion were not together at all during this time but in constant communication. Greene was still in the upstate dealing with small Redcoat outposts. Marion, likewise, was suppressing small British garrisons in "the neck" along the South Carolina coast north of Charleston.

But the situation with both their armies was desperate. There was little food, no clothes for the coming winter and almost no ammunition.

Fortunately, supplies and, more importantly, back pay soon arrived, courtesy of John Laurens' successful mission to France. The mood improved and Marion contemplated his next move.

Greene prepared to move against Charleston, joining with Marion's forces. John Laurens quickly rejoined Greene after Yorktown, once again, riding alongside the now famous Swamp Fox. Samuel Huger was at his side.

By the end of October, Greene was able to assemble 4,000 men, mostly South Carolina militia and, with several hundred mounted Continentals, moved on Dorchester, about15 miles from Charleston. The small British garrison there fled to the safety of Charleston.

The British had reluctantly consolidated their resources in the south within Charleston, and Greene and Marion began planning another assault. At this point, John Laurens resurrected his earlier proposal to arm slaves and have them join Greene's Army. His abolitionist views, first conceived during his education in Paris, were further intensified by his wartime experience. But the proposal would have to be approved by the South Carolina Governor John Rutledge, just back from his exile.

The proposal was quickly debated and, predictably, failed to be approved.

Greene positioned some of his men south of the city to ensure no supplies or reinforcements came up from Savannah. Charleston was soon surrounded by the Continental Army and the South Carolina militia under Francis Marion. Throughout November, desperate British raids were held outside of the city as they foraged for food. They burned every building they encountered on their way back.

On December 12, a mounted column of Americans led by Francis Marion entered Charleston. The few British guards abandoned their posts, retreating down to the waterfront. These men had no stomach for any more fighting.

The city was eerily quiet, the streets deserted. Marion's men, nearly all South Carolinians, were shocked at how their beloved city had been destroyed. As the British were evacuating, they told the citizens to stay indoors. Hundreds of slaves were held in filthy jails. Dysentery was rampant throughout the city, due to the lack of clean drinking water.

The American soldiers encouraged the people to come out of their homes.

A short time later, General Greene alongside General Moultrie, who had been imprisoned two years earlier when Charleston surrendered, rode into the city at the head of a large, mounted column of Continentals. The people slowly emerged, standing on corners and balconies waving to the Continental Army. Charleston was in ruins, its economy shattered. But their city had been liberated.

There were no further hostilities from either side. Over the next few months, more than 40 ships carried what was left of the British Army out and up to New York. With them were nearly 4,000 loyalists, South Carolina citizens who feared retribution from the Americans. The fine plantation owners' homes, including that of Henry Laurens, had been occupied for two years by British officers and were all in ruins. On their way out, the British looted whatever they could … silver, paintings, even the church bells of St. Michael's.

Chapter 51 ~ The Last Man to Die

What began in January 1782 in South Carolina can only be viewed as a tragedy. As the British Parliament was debating how to gracefully exit the conflict in America, dozens of small loyalist backwoods groups in North and South Carolina reorganized to resist the American Army. A series of small, bloody battles were fought in remote places.

A remaining British garrison on John's Island was assaulted, unsuccessfully, by American General Harry Lee in January 1782. In North Carolina, partisan loyalists, such as David Fanning and "Bloody Bill" Cunningham, conducted months long acts of terrorism on their American neighbors. Hundreds died. Prisoners were hung or shot.

It was August 1782 before Great Britain officially notified Washington of their intent to cease all hostilities.

But one final blow to American leadership was yet to happen. Before dawn on August 26, 150 Redcoats, facing starvation, came ashore in Beaufort, just north of Savannah. They were on a desperate foraging party, and a local farmer brought word during the night to Laurens' camp. John Laurens was in command of about only fifty Continental soldiers, including Lieutenant Samuel Huger.

Waking his men, Lieutenant Laurens, was impatient for a fight.

Sam tried to warn him.

"John, don't do this, we don't know how many there are and our ammunition is very low. Let's wait for reinforcements."

"No, Sam, we are going. This has to stop."

It would be their last conversation.

Jumping on his horse, Laurens led his thin column into the pre-dawn darkness. A few minutes later, a single shot rang out. Lieutenant Colonel John Laurens was shot, falling from his mount.

A junior officer who came to his aid was also killed. Samuel Huger dragged both behind a nearby fence but could not save either man. John lived for a few minutes in Samuel's arms, his eyes wide open.

Word of Laurens' death quickly spread and was reported up the line. When Washington learned of it a week later, he wept. John's father was still in London recovering from his jailing and was inconsolable when, months later, learned of the death of his son. He wrote to a friend,

"*Thank God I had such a son, who dared to die for his country.*"

John Adams, perhaps, said it best, "*Colonel John Laurens, age 28, the last man to die in the American Revolution.*"

Chapter 52 ~ After the War

It was April 1783, 18 months after Yorktown, before Congress would officially declare an end to the war. The Treaty of Paris was signed in September with an ailing Ben Franklin presiding. The war had been fought over eight years and in hundreds of locations from Maine to Georgia. Much of the American countryside had been destroyed and the American economy, so strong in 1775, was at a trickle. Cities like Charleston and Savannah were in ruins.

The men who fought, returned home to their farms and villages, putting away their muskets and uniforms. These "citizen-soldiers" would now go back to their families and their former way of life.

The main characters in our story would go on with their lives.

Alexander Hamilton had always intended to have a career in the new American government. He wrote to his friend John Laurens on August 15, 1782, "*Quit your sword, my friend, put on your toga, and come to Congress.*"

Two weeks later, Laurens was dead.

Hamilton had been at General Washington's side since the Battle of Trenton in December 1776 and would go on to a major leadership role under Washington as the country's first Secretary of the Treasury. He took on the Herculean task of managing the country's finances at a time when there was no financial infrastructure. He served under Washington for many more years and can be credited for getting the bankrupt country back on its feet.

He died in a duel with Aaron Burr in 1804 in New Jersey.

The Marquis de Lafayette returned home to France in January 1782 to a hero's welcome. He was happily rejoined with his wife Adrienne who had patiently waited for him all those years. They had two more children, and he was welcomed with open arms at the Court of King Louis. Washington wrote him in late 1782 to inform him of the death of John Laurens.

He traveled back to America twice in the years immediately after the war and, on both occasions, was afforded a hero's welcome. He was awarded US citizenship in 1783 and, on one of the trips, he became friends with James Madison, a friendship that lasted for many years. Lafayette believed strongly in the words of the Declaration of Independence and took up his friend John Laurens' cause for emancipation. In 1783, he formally proposed to Washington that, together, they purchase a plantation with blacks as salaried tenants. Washington politely excused himself from the proposal saying that the time was not right.

Lafayette traveled extensively throughout the colonies visiting New York, Philadelphia, Richmond, and Charleston. He even spent time in Yorktown observing the craters and trenches from the siege. In December 1784, he visited Washington at Mount Vernon. After they parted, Washington wrote to Lafayette.

"I have often asked myself, as our carriages distended, whether that was the last sight I should ever have of you. And though I wish to say no, my fears say yes."

Lafayette wrote back, *"No, my beloved general, my late parting was not by any means a last interview …"*

Washington's premonition was correct as they never saw each other again. It would be another 40 years before Lafayette would return to America, and George Washington would die in 1799.

[Duncan, 159-160]

John Laurens (1754-1782) There is no man who had a broader impact on the birth of America than John Laurens. The son of one of the wealthiest men in America, he used his money and position to further the causes of liberty and emancipation. He fought in nearly every battle that involved George Washington. He then traveled to his home state of South Carolina when it was threatened. He fought at Savannah and Charleston where he was captured. Once released, he was sent to France to negotiate on America's behalf with the French. Had he not been successful in convincing King Louis to come to the financial aid of America, Yorktown would never have happened. He led a battlefield assault on Yorktown in October 1781. He died in 1782 in a meaningless skirmish with British soldiers who were foraging for food at a time when the war was clearly over. It is said that Washington openly wept when he learned of John Laurens' death.

He was buried at his family home, Mepkin Plantation on the Cooper River, outside of Charleston. He was married and had one child in London that he had never met.

He was 27 years old when he died.

Francis Marion (1732-1795) The Swamp Fox was, perhaps, the most legendary of all the Revolutionary War heroes. Born the same year as George Washington, he became a member of the South Carolina militia at a relatively old age. He first distinguished himself at Charleston in 1776 but came to Washington's attention very late in the war. Having driven Cornwallis north to Virginia in the summer of 1781, Marion was not present at Yorktown, riding with Nathanael Greene in South Carolina.

After the war, he returned to his farm near Georgetown and married his cousin, Mary Esther Videau. He was elected to the South Carolina assembly, and, in 1790, he participated in writing the South Carolina Constitution.

He retired from public life and died on his plantation, Pond Bluff, in 1795. He was buried on his brother Gabriel's plantation, Belle Isle.

General Nathanael Greene (1742-1786) A Rhode Island native, he was a leader throughout the war and at Washington's side in all the critical engagements. He was instrumental in the South Carolina conflicts of 1781 and 1782, replacing General Horatio Gates, after the rout at Camden. He led the retaking of Charleston in December 1781. When the war finally ended, he dismissed his Army and headed north, leaving South Carolina. He stopped for a hero's welcome in Wilmington, Richmond, and Baltimore before joining Washington in Princeton. He submitted his resignation to Congress and returned home to his family in Rhode Island.

He soon moved to Georgia and established a plantation on land given to him as thanks by the Georgia legislature. He died there in 1786 on what is called Mulberry Grove Plantation in Chatham County.

Benjamin Huger (1746-1779) He was a real-life figure in the Revolutionary War and is the father of our fictional character Samuel Huger. Benjamin was born at Limerick Plantation, South Carolina, fourth son of Daniel and Mary (Cordes) Huger. One of the celebrated Patriot Huger brothers, grandsons of Daniel Huger, the refugee from France. Benjamin was educated in Europe with his brothers, was a representative in the commons house of the assembly of South Carolina and, along with his brothers Isaac and John, was a delegate to the provincial congress in 1775. He joined his brothers in encouraging Revolutionary movement in South Carolina and was commissioned Major of the 1st Regiment of Riflemen, afterward the 5th South Carolina regiment in the continental establishment.

While engaged in reconnoitering the position of the British under Prevost before Charleston, he was shot and killed by friendly fire on May 11, 1779.

Benjamin Huger was buried in St. Philip's Church cemetery in Charleston.

Inscription:

Sacred to the Memory of
MAJOR BENJAMIN HUGER,
Who fell before the Lines of Charleston,
On the 11th day of May 1779,
In the thirty-second year of his Age.

Henry Laurens (1724-1792) Prior to the war, he was one of the wealthiest men in America, the owner of eight plantations in South Carolina. He was a major rice and indigo producer and a slave trader. He married and had 11 children but his wife and eight of his children died in the 1770s. John Laurens was his oldest surviving son. Henry was elected President of the Continental Congress in 1777 and served until 1780.

He was then commissioned as Minister to Holland. He was captured by the British, traveling to Holland in September 1780, imprisoned in the Tower of London, and exchanged for General Cornwallis in 1781. He recovered his health and returned home to find his plantation home burned to the ground. He lived out his years in a smaller house on the grounds until his death in 1792. He requested in his will that he be cremated and his ashes spread across his South Carolina land.

Today, his plantation home is the site of Mepkin Abbey and Botanical Garden, near Moncks Corner, owned by the Catholic Trappist monks.

General William Moultrie (1730-1805) An American general in the Continental Army, he successfully defended Charleston with Francis Marion in 1776. He was captured with the fall of Charleston in 1780 and held prisoner until Yorktown.

After independence, Moultrie advanced as a South Carolina politician. He was elected by the legislature twice within a decade as Governor (1785-1787, 1792-1794), serving two terms. (The state constitution kept power in the hands of the legislature and prohibited governors from serving two terms in succession.)

After the war, the fort he and Francis Marion had defended was formally named Fort Moultrie. During that attack by the British in 1776, a flag he had designed was flown – a field of blue bearing a white crescent with the word LIBERTY on it. The flag was shot down during the fight. It became an icon of the Revolution in the south and was named "*The Moultrie.*" The state of South Carolina has incorporated that design into its current state flag.

William Moultrie died in 1805 after publishing his memoirs in 1802.

General Henry Clinton (1730-1795) A career military officer, he fought in the Seven Years War and arrived in Boston in 1778 in time for the skirmish at Bunker Hill. He was given leave to return home in 1777 but sent back to replace Lord Howe in New York in 1778. It was he who was charged with implementing the *Southern Strategy.*

In 1783, he published a "*Narrative of the Campaign of 1781 in North America*" in which he blamed Cornwallis for the failures against the Americans. A very public dispute with Cornwallis ensued.

In 1790, he was elected to Parliament and then was appointed Governor of Gibraltar but died before he could assume that post.

General Cornwallis (1738-1805) He was from an aristocratic English family and educated at Cambridge and Eton. He joined the British Army as a young man, rising steadily through the ranks. After the fall of Charleston in 1780, he was placed in charge of the *Southern Strategy* by Henry Clinton and wreaked havoc all across South Carolina, soundly defeating General Horatio Gates at Camden. Cornwallis surrendered his Army to Washington and Rochambeau at Yorktown in 1781. He was held prisoner and exchanged for Henry Laurens in December 1781.

Despite the defeat at Yorktown, he served as Military Governor in Ireland and later in India. He died in India in 1805.

Banastre Tarleton (1754-1833) He was the British Lieutenant-Colonel operating under the command of Cornwallis in South Carolina. The son of a prosperous sugar trader, he was educated at Oxford and purchased a commission in the British Army at age 21. He first came to the attention of British military leaders when he captured the American General Charles Lee in New Jersey in 1776. He became notorious for his extreme behavior, torturing and killing Americans and burning homes and businesses in the south. He famously pursued, unsuccessfully, Francis Marion for nearly two years in South Carolina.

He was wounded (losing three fingers) in the defense of Gloucester Point across the river from Yorktown in that notable battle, captured, paroled and sent home to England. At age 27, his active military career was over. He was later elected to British Parliament using his war wounds as a campaign asset.

He died in 1833 at the age of 79.

Benedict Arnold (1740-1801) After his infamous defection to the British, Clinton assigned him to Virginia as a Brigadier General where he conducted a reign of terror that included destroying much of Richmond. Lafayette pursued him in 1781 but could not capture him.

After the war, he and his wife moved to London where he was greeted with mixed reactions. He and Peggy eventually moved to Canada where he started a merchant business with their son. But his negative reputation preceded him and they returned to London in 1791.

He died in 1801 at the age of 61.

Sources and References

Crawford, Allen Pell, *This Fierce People – The Untold Story of America's Revolutionary War in the South*, 2024, Alfred P. Knopf, New York.

Duncan, Mike, *Hero of Two Worlds – The Marquis de Lafayette in the Age of Revolution*, 2021, Hachette Book Group, New York.

Edgar, Walter Z., *Partisans and Redcoats*, 2001, Harper Collins Publishers, New York.

Greene, Jerome A., *The Guns of Independence – The Siege of Yorktown*, 2005, Savas Beatie, California.

Oller, John, *The Swamp Fox*, 2016, Hachette Book Group, New York.

McAlister, Robert, *Georgetown's North Island*, 2015, History Press, Charleston, SC.

Unger, Harlow Giles, *The Last Man To Die In The American Revolution*, 2023, independently published.

Weir, Robert W., *Colonial South Carolina – A History*, 1983, 1997, University of South Carolina Press.

Zucker, A. E., *General DeKalb, Lafayette's Mentor*, 1966, May 2020, University of North Carolina Press.

Illustrations

Yorktown Gallery

THE BRITISH

King George III
by Allan Ramsey
Buckingham Palace
Royal Trust

These two men were responsible for the war against the colonies from 1775-1783. Germain had the title of Foreign Minister and corresponded with his Generals on strategy in North America frequently.

The British Parliament was divided during this time weighing the cost of the war against British rule. King George was a supporter of the war and tried unsuccessfully to keep the French from getting involved.

Lord Charles Germain
Library of Congress

These three British generals led the war in the American colonies.

Lord Richard Howe
National Portrait Gallery

Lord Howe enjoyed early success at the Battle of Brooklyn in 1776 but was surprised at Trenton and Princeton by Washington in December of that year. He was removed when he decided to abandon Burgoyne leading to the British defeat at Ticonderoga.

Henry Clinton took over and defeated Washington at Brandywine in 1777 and the siege of Charleston in 1780.

Henry Clinton
by Andrea Soldi
American Museum in Britain

Cornwallis was responsible for "The Southern Strategy" on the ground in the south and surrendered his entire army of 7000 men at Yorktown in 1781.

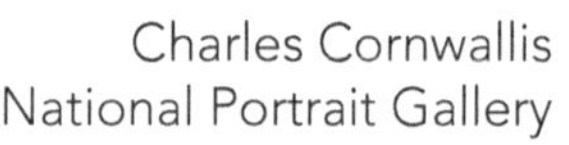

Charles Cornwallis
National Portrait Gallery

Lieutenant-Colonel
Banastre Tarleton
by Sir Joshua Reynolds
National Portrait Gallery

Tarleton rose through the ranks for his leadership at Brooklyn and Brandywine and was sent south with Cornwallis. He was notorious for his vicious tactics and was ordered to track down and kill or capture Francis Marion, calling him "The Swamp Fox." He tried unsuccessfully for two years.

THE AMERICANS

Henry Laurens
by Lemuel Francis Abbott
National Portrait Gallery

Henry Laurens was a wealthy plantation owner in South Carolina who was elected as President of the Continental Congress in 1777. He was the father of John Laurens. Henry was captured by the British in 1780 on his way to Holland so sign a treaty with the Dutch. He spent the reminder of the war in the Tower of London as a prisoner.

General William Moultrie
National Portrait Gallery

General William Moultrie was a South Carolina plantation owner and commanding general of the South Carolina militia. He was an early mentor to Francis Marion and successfully defended Charleston against Clinton and the British in 1776. He was later taken prisoner in 1780 when Charleston fell. Washington afforded him the honor of accepting Cornwallis' surrender at Yorktown.

General Benedict Arnold
National Portrait Gallery

The infamous American General was wounded and the hero at Ticonderoga but felt that Washington was not paying him enough respect. He defected to the British in a failed attempt to turn over West Point in 1779. Washington assigned Lafayette to track down Arnold in Virginia in 1781. He was in New York with Clinton when Yorktown fell and soon after that, sailed for England with his wife.

Francis Marion
National Portrait Gallery

Francis Marion was the most enigmatic of all of the American military leaders during the War of Independence. Severely premature at birth, his growth was stunted, and he walked with a limp his entire life, He was a farmer in 1775 before joining the South Carolina militia. He defeated Clinton's siege of Charleston in 1776 and was present at the unsuccessful American siege of Savannah in 1780. When his commanding officer Horatio Gates abandoned him in 1780, he was left on his own with a small band of men to defend South Carolina. Cornwallis assigned several companies of British Redcoats to capture or kill Marion. His nickname "The Swamp Fox" came from his ability to elude the British 1778-1781.

WASHINGTON'S "THREE SONS"

Alexander Hamilton
by Charles Turnbull
National Portrait Gallery

Gilbert Marquis de Lafayette
by Charles Boze
National Portrait Gallery

John Laurens
by Charles Wilson Peale
National Portrait Gallery

George Washington
by Charles Wilson Peale
National Portrait Galllery

About The Author

This is Thomas W. Lee's second novel about the American Revolution. The first book, published in March 2023, *The Chatham Patriot*, told the story of America's struggle for independence through the eyes of a fictional seventeen-year-old in the village of Chatham, New Jersey.

The author's friends in his hometown of Pawleys Island, South Carolina, encouraged him to write about the events of that era in the Palmetto State. One day in June 2023, he passed a small historical marker just north of Georgetown, South Carolina. It read simply *"Lafayette, a lover of Liberty, left France … and arrived at Benjamin Huger's summer home near here in June 1777."*

That sign piqued Lee's curiosity, and he began to research. What he found was a rich story that began with Lafayette's arrival, the siege of Charleston in 1778, and the exploits of a unique South Carolina militia officer. Told through the eyes of the fictional son of plantation owner Benjamin Huger, *The Palmetto Patriot* recounts the British attempt to subdue South Carolina 1778-1781 and march north to trap George Washington.

The story recounts the exploits of Lafayette and John Laurens, two of Washington's closest aides. Laurens was born on his father's South Carolina plantation, captured at Charleston, paroled and dispatched by Washington to the Court of French King Louis XVI to plead America's cause. Laurens returned with supplies, armaments, and French money to equip and pay the beleaguered American Continental soldiers, leading to the pivotal victory at Yorktown in 1781.

Written for both younger readers and adults who want to know more about this little known chapter in the American Revolution, *The Palmetto Patriot* also tells the story of Francis Marion, the famous "Swamp Fox," as the British generals called him. After Charleston fell, this diminutive militia officer and his small group of men were the last thing stopping the British advance north in 1779-1780.

Thomas Lee can be reached at thomaslee@sc.rr.com.

These are the times that try men's souls. The summer soldier and the sunshine patriot will, in this crisis, shrink from the service of their country; but he that stands by it now, deserves the love and thanks of man and woman. Tyranny, like hell, is not easily conquered; yet we have this consolation with us, that the harder the conflict, the more glorious the triumph. What we obtain too cheap, we esteem too lightly: it is dearness only that gives everything its value. Heaven knows how to put a proper price upon its goods; and it would be strange indeed if so celestial an article as freedom should not be highly rated. Britain, with an army to enforce her tyranny, has declared that she has a right (not only to TAX) but "to bind us in all cases whatsoever" and if being bound in that manner, is not slavery, then is there not such a thing as slavery upon earth. Even the expression is impious; for so unlimited a power can belong only to God.

Thomas Paine
December 23, 1776

217

www.ingramcontent.com/pod-product-compliance
Lightning Source LLC
Chambersburg PA
CBHW040526170726
48295CB00012B/359